The Threshold of Worlds
A Novel by

Hichem Karoui

Global East-West. London

Contents

"The abstraction of the desert landscape cleansed me, and rendered my mind vacant with its superfluous greatness; a greatness achieved not by the addition of thought to its emptiness, but by its substraction."

T.E. Lawrence: Seven Pillars of Wisdom

One

Prologue

Shadows of the Past and the Threshold's Whisper

As the fading light cast long shadows across the Dorset landscape, Ahmed found himself ensnared in a labyrinth of shadows and echoes that refused to fade. The air grew thick with a stillness that whispered of secrets long buried beneath the moss and heather, yet thrummed with an undercurrent of restless energy. The genteel beauty of the approaching dusk disguised the silent tension mounting in his chest, each breath a shallow echo of his mounting quandary. His mind, a whirl of conflicting perceptions, struggled to reconcile rational doubts with the strange certainty that had begun to take root. Somewhere between skepticism and a visceral sense of unseen currents, he sensed that the fabric of history itself was rippling, fraying at the edges like a worn tapestry pulled taut by time's relentless hand.

The breakdown of his car near Clouds Hill proved more than mere mechanical misfortune; it appeared a deliberate sign, a rupture in his journey that beckoned him further into the unknown. The cottage that emerged from the shadows was unlike any structure he had anticipated—rambling, cloaked in ivy and shadow, its windows glowing with a warm, inviting light that bespoke secrets beyond this world. Ahmed hesitated, feeling the weight of centuries pressing upon his shoulders as he approached. The garden, overgrown yet alive, seemed to pulse with a silent vitality, as if guarding stories too immense to be spoken aloud. The sense of being watched, yet welcomed, infused the moment with a strange double-edged clarity—an invitation and a warning simultaneously echoing in the cool evening breeze.

Outside, the figure upon the veranda was an apparition, her bearing reminiscent of aristocratic grace refined through generations. Lady Edith Carrington's composure, a slow measured grace, contrasted sharply with the wild tangled landscape behind her. Her eyes held depths that beckoned to an unfathomable part of Ahmed—glinting with secret knowledge and a thousand unspoken truths. With measured poise, she rose from her seat, extending a delicate hand that seemed to pulse with subtle energy, as if she carried within her the weight of uncounted histories. Her words flowed softly but carried the authority of someone whose existence transcended mere time; she welcomed him as though expecting him from some distant, impossible past. There was an almost musical cadence to her speech, a rhythm that seemed to dance between the lines of reality and myth, forcing Ahmed to question whether he stood within the confines of his understanding or at the threshold of something far greater.

The interior revealed a sanctuary of curiosities that defied the modest exterior, each object whispering secrets of an otherwise unseen universe. Shelves lined with first editions of Burton's Arabian Nights and Doughty's Arabia Deserta hinted at a passion for stories that bridged centuries and cultures. Persian miniatures, intricate in their detail, seemed to shimmer with silent life, whispering histories that stretched beyond the confines of known time. Silverware that carried the patina of ages past decorated the shelves—each piece seemingly an artifact of some long-forgotten ritual or clandestine meeting. Ahmed's eyes lingered on these relics, each one hinting at a deeper layer of reality, a realm where history and consciousness intertwined in ways he had only theorized. Lady Edith served a cup of tea—rare Pu-erh, she claimed, a gift from "Ned," a name that resonated cryptically in the sacred quiet of this hidden world. Her voice, soothing yet layered with the weight of personal history, challenged Ahmed's assumptions, drawing him into an intimate dialogue that blurred the boundaries between historian and mystic.

As the night deepened, Edith's stories began to unfold like delicate silk threads woven through the fabric of time itself. She painted vivid images of Lawrence—recalling nights when his restless pacing would fill the room as he recited passages from the Quran in flawless Arabic while Sassoon scribbled frantically and Augustus John sketched his errant movements. Her voice carried the echo of distant cups of coffee, heated debates that stretched until dawn, and the volatile energy of a man forever chasing an elusive truth. Edith's descriptions hinted that Lawrence's retreat to Clouds Hill was more than a physical escape; it was an act of probing the very fabric of possibility, seeking gateways beyond the linear confines of history. She claimed that Lawrence had uncovered the existence of "temporal anomalies," places where time wavered like a candle in a draft—locations where past and future could be glimpsed in fleeting moments, where memories could bleed into the present like ink into water. The very landscape of Dorset, she insisted, was woven with these threads, waiting for the right observer to unravel its secrets.

With the slow unveiling of Lawrence's journals, the room grew heavier with revelation. Edith handed Ahmed a leather-bound volume, its appearance aged but the handwriting unmistakably Lawrence's—sharp, deliberate, infused with an unyielding clarity that defied mere scribbling. The words within were more than military notes—they were an outcry of consciousness itself. Reports of "displacement events," references to "chronological flux," and sketches of unrecognizable aerial craft hinted at secrets veiled behind the accepted narratives. The journals spoke of "higher states of awareness," of portals that could be open at specific points in space and time, driven by the human mind's capacity to transcend the ordinary. Ahmed, engrossed and unnerved, was struck by the intensity of the scientific tone, which contrasted sharply with the poetic rhythm of the handwriting—whispering that Lawrence had perceived reality as layers—a complex mosaic of overlapping dimensions awaiting discovery.

Perhaps the most startling revelation was Edith's explanation of the true meaning behind the phrase "To S.A.," inscribed so famously in Seven Pillars of Wisdom. She detailed how the initials referred, not to a person or simple dedication, but to "Sahra Al-Zaman"—the Desert of Time—a mystical locus where the boundaries of history dissolve. According to Edith, Lawrence's experiences revealed that certain earthly locations contain "currents"—powerful, invisible streams where time flows unevenly, allowing glimpses into possible futures and alternate realities. The desert, vast and silent, embodied this principle—a place where consciousness could stretch, fold, and transform. She claimed that Lawrence's obsession was driven by his discovery of these "currents," and that his retreat into the landscape was more than a withdrawal from war; it was a quest to understand the very essence of existence—an attempt to forge a bridge between the mortal and the divine.

As the clock neared 3:17 AM—the time Edith called "Lawrence's hour"—a shift in the atmosphere announced the commencement of something beyond comprehension. The air vibrated with a subtle resonance, a harmonic frequency felt rather than heard, curling around Ahmed's consciousness and dissolving the distinctions between self and surroundings. Outside, the sky above Clouds Hill fractured like ancient parchment—brilliant fissures of light rippled through the heavens, revealing forms impossible to describe. An entity emerged, a being of pure luminance that shimmered like liquid silver and yet bore an uncanny resemblance to human shape—tall, graceful, evolving beyond the limits of biological form. Its presence shimmered as if reality itself was momentarily unraveling, exposing the fragile threads that held worlds together.

The luminous beings communicated directly—thought by thought, emotion by emotion—an exchange that swept through Ahmed's mind. Their voices were distant yet intimate, reverberating in a language that transcended words, yet seemed familiar in the innermost corners of consciousness. They identified themselves as custodians of the evolving human awareness, guardians of the fragile thresholds where worlds intersect. Their message was both a warning and a summons—a whisper of impending change, a reminder that Earth teetered on the verge of a profound shift in its very fabric. Humanity, they explained, had long been guided by those who could navigate these currents—heroes, mystics, visionaries—and now, perhaps, a new guardian had been chosen. Ahmed felt an overwhelming tide of understanding rush over him: the universe was not a static place but a liquid ocean, a place where consciousness, not matter, shaped reality.

In that moment of cosmic revelation, Ahmed's senses expanded beyond ordinary limits. Time folded and unfolded like a complex origami—possibility streams branching into infinite configurations. The beings revealed that Earth's future was contingent on recognition—on awareness of these hidden currents and the ability to transcend the illusion of linearity. They showed him a universe of multiple probabilities, each one a ripple in the eternal sea, where humanity's consciousness could ascend or descend into chaos. Lawrence, in this shadowy pantheon of higher entities, was a guide—an agent who had glimpsed these depths and sought to prepare others for the moment when the currents would converge. Ahmed's own journey, woven into this cosmic fabric, evolved into a calling to serve as a bridge—an interpreter—between worlds that had long remained unseen.

When dawn's first light spilled into the ruins, Ahmed awoke with a start, as if thrown back into the material realm by an act of cosmic necessity. The landscape appeared unchanged, yet everything had shifted within him. Clutched in his hands was a fragment—a tiny crystalline object pulsing with an inner light, cooling in his palm as if alive with consciousness itself. The distant echoes of luminous voices still lingered in his mind, whispering truths too vast for words. As he examined the relic, the realization washed over him: his role was no longer confined to scholarship or history. It was to carry the memory of Lawrence, the knowledge of the currents, and the responsibility to guide humanity across the threshold—into the infinite possibilities awaiting beyond the veil of linear time. The awakening had begun, and with it, the dawning of a new era—one in which consciousness itself would shape the destiny of the universe.

***

The evening descended with a quiet heaviness, as the Dorset sky settled into shades of deep violet and ink, cloaking the land in a silence so profound it seemed to hold its breath. The heathland stretched out like a restless ocean, rolling hills and gorse bushes wavering under a wind that carried whispers older than memory itself. Ahmed sat silently in his car, the engine dead—a sudden, inexplicable failure—and stared at the blackened horizon, feeling a strange tremor beneath his skin. This landscape was no ordinary moor; it thrummed with unseen forces, as if the land itself preserved stories of forgotten worlds, waiting for someone to listen.

He remembered how the myths clung to the air here, woven into every gust and shadow. The legends of realm-travelers, of spectral figures wandering the misty brambles, and of ancient anchors binding these fields to worlds beyond human sight. His rational mind, trained in the rigorous pursuit of historical truth, struggled against an instinctive pull—a feeling that this place was a threshold, a thin membrane dividing worlds that had long ago touched and retreated. The land seemed to pulse with memories; ghostly echoes of armies dispatched and secrets buried beneath layers of history and myth, each whisper hinting that Dorset's surface was a veneer masking deeper currents of time and consciousness.

As the darkness thickened, Ahmed felt a shift within. The landscape seemed to breathe, exhaling an ancient sigh, and he grew aware—perhaps for the first time—that this is where stories that defy linear reality had their roots. Time here was not a steady march but a fluid, shape-shifting tapestry, threads pulling and twisting in ways that challenged every scientific principle he held dear. His mind, ever hungry for rational clarity, grappled with the sense of invisible pathways opening, guiding him toward something beyond words—an invitation to glimpse the stories woven into Dorset's silent stones, stories that shimmered just beneath the surface like mirages formed from memory and myth intertwined.

Behind him, the approach of dusk and the subtle flickering of lights in the undergrowth seemed to beckon him closer to the mystery. Each shadow appeared as a fragment of a larger puzzle, fragmented images of a reality that once whispered through the ages—of figures who traversed these very fields long before modern memory recorded their names. Ahmed's skin prickled with a strange awareness: the land was alive with consciousness, conscious of him now, as if it recognized a seeker arriving at its sacred boundary. His pulse quickened; he knew, instinctively, that crossing this threshold would unfold truths considered impossible within the confines of his disciplined worldview.

Then, almost imperceptibly, the landscape grew still, as if holding its breath in anticipation. A mist curled through the heather—a gossamer veil crawling between the ancient oaks and the battered remnants of forgotten structures—drawing nearer like a shroud of time itself. The sense of unseen forces gathering sharpened, and a gentle, almost imperceptible hum resonated in his mind, a melody of remembrance deeper than sound. It was as if Dorset's very essence was awakening, summoning him to a space where memory and myth blurred into a single, unbreakable chain—an invisible thread linking present and past, reality and legend, in the dance of shadows that refused to be fully cast away by his reason.

Suddenly, a faint glow pierced the gloom—a soft, golden flicker emanating from behind a copse of silver birch and rhododendrons—like the faint pulse of some distant heart trying to communicate. Ahmed's gaze fixed on the light, feeling his body tighten with an awareness that a memory long repressed was awakening. Was it warning him? Or calling him forward? The boundary he suspected existed between worlds was thinning, a delicate membrane that shimmered under the weight of stories waiting for the right observer—someone unburdened by disbelief, someone who dared to step beyond the edge of accepted reality. In that moment, with each breath, he understood that Dorset's mythic energy wasn't merely folklore—here, memory and myth had fused into a living force, waiting for him to acknowledge its presence and understand its whisper.

***

Under the pale glow of the dying sun, the Dorset landscape stretched out like an ancient manuscript, its silent hills and restless heathlands whispering secrets to the wind. Ahmed's car had come to a halt at the edge of a wilderness he once thought familiar, yet now felt strangely alien, as if the land itself had shifted in the twilight hours. His fingers trembled as he turned the ignition key, the engine dying with a final, sluggish groan—a surrender to forces beyond his comprehension. He stepped out into the cooling air, sensing that the moment of ordinary disconnection was merely the threshold into something far more profound. Behind him, the landscape seemed to breathe, shadows lengthening and dissolving into the velvet dusk, whispering echoes of stories long buried beneath the surface of time.

Walking toward the darkened silhouette of Clouds Hill, Ahmed felt a peculiar pull—an almost visceral sensation that this was no longer mere wilderness but a place where the fabric of reality had thinned. Instead of the expected cottage, his eyes caught the outline of a rambling structure, its architecture speaking of a bygone era—Arts and Crafts, yet somehow imbued with a subtle pulsation, as if it breathed in tandem with the land itself. The windows spilled warmth into the evening gloom, inviting and mysterious. As he approached the veranda, a figure emerged—an elderly woman whose posture bore the weight of aristocratic grace and silent knowing. Her gaze, steady and penetrating, held Ahmed as if she had been awaiting him across the unseen veil of centuries, her presence a doorway into truths seldom spoken yet deeply felt.

Her name was Lady Edith Carrington, a name that evoked a sense of faded grandeur and unspoken histories. She offered him a seat and a cup of tea, the steam rising in fragrant wisps, filling the air with an aroma that beckoned memories of distant lands. The interior defied modest expectations; shelves lined with first editions—Doughty's Arabia Deserta nestling alongside Burton's Nights, Persian miniatures glittering amid Bedouin silver—each artifact a fragment of a story woven into the very walls. Lady Edith's voice, cultivated and gentle, carried a weight of centuries; she spoke with an intimacy that suggested years not of age, but of accumulated experience. Her words seemed to dance between shadow and light, revealing glimpses of a hidden history that challenged Ahmed's rational worldview, speaking softly of gatherings where Lawrence recited passages from the Quran, his voice merging with the crackle of the fire, or of fierce debates that stretched into the dawn—debates that, in their essence, fought not just over land, but over the very nature of time itself.

As her stories unfolded—shedding light on Lawrence's private meetings with Sassoon and the portraits of unsung figures—Ahmed's skepticism began to erode. Edith produced Lawrence's journals, their leather covers aged yet meticulously preserved, with pages filled with handwritten notes that spat in the face of orthodox history. The handwriting, unmistakably Lawrence's, captivated him—details describing "chronological displacement events," theories of consciousness that transcended linear time, and sketches of strange crafts that defied all known engineering principles. The air thickened with the weight of revelation, as Edith revealed that Lawrence's retreat to Clouds Hill was far more than an escape from duty; it was a carefully concealed investigation into phenomena that stretched the boundaries of understanding, rooted in the landscape's ancient power and whispered through the fabric of the universe itself.

The conversation turned toward a mysterious dedication in "Seven Pillars of Wisdom": "To S.A." For years, scholars had attributed it to a person or a simple abbreviation, but Edith's voice quivered with certainty as she unveiled the truth—Sahra Al-Zaman, "The Desert of Time." She explained that Lawrence, through encounters in the desert sands, had uncovered locations that resonated with hidden currents, where the very essence of time could ripple and bend. These points in the Earth's crust, she claimed, are gateways—not merely physical terrains but portals into the depths of consciousness, where past, present, and future dissolve into one unfolding tapestry. The desert, long dismissed as an arid expanse, was, in fact, a living nexus that had revealed to Lawrence the malleable nature of temporal flow—a truth buried beneath myth and history, waiting to be rediscovered by those ready to see beyond the surface.

As darkness descended, Edith's words gained a luminous quality, her voice waxing in rhythm with the slowly deepening night. She spoke of her role as a guardian—an ancient keeper of one such nexus—who had been witness to sights beyond human memory from childhood, moments when the landscape had flickered and shimmered with unseen energy. Lawrence's true mission, she claimed, extended far beyond the Arab Revolt; it was a quest to understand and safeguard these intersections, gateways where the fabric of reality was porous and malleable. She described beings—luminous and tall—whose presence suggested evolution to heights beyond human imagining, entities that communicated directly through shared consciousness, their thoughts flowing into Ahmed's mind, languages blending seamlessly as if they had existed forever within the infinite of thought itself. They explained that Earth was approaching a critical point—an evolutionary leap—and that Lawrence, in his own way, had been a pioneer navigating these currents long before the world caught wind of his exploits.

The night's chill deepened, yet Ahmed felt a warmth—an awakening that refused to be denied. Edith's stories grew more abstract, describing a realm where form was fluid and consciousness was the primary architect of existence. He saw visions of Earth's many futures, some shining with cosmic awareness, others darkened by chaos, in which mankind's refusal or readiness to step into the infinite would determine its fate. It dawned on him that these gateways were not relics of the past but living portals—vessels waiting for the right minds to activate their potential. He sensed that Lawrence's true seizure of the desert was less about military conquest and more about seizing the moment when human awareness could pierce through the illusions of time and space, awakening to a broader reality.

When the clock struck exactly 3:17 AM—a moment Edith called "Lawrence's hour"—the landscape around Clouds Hill shifted perceptibly. A harmonic resonance, subtle yet undeniable, vibrated through the air like a tuning fork of the universe. Hovering above the peak was a craft of impossible beauty, its surface flickering between states—part metal, part liquid light, shimmering with unnameable hues. It seemed to exist in multiple dimensions at once, defying the limitations of visual perception, a symbol of the unseen currents that Lawrence had traced and now, in some mysterious way, Ahmed was being invited to join. Tall luminous beings emerged from the craft, their forms conveying a sense of timeless evolution. Their presence pulsed with an intensity that bypassed words—an intelligence that poured directly into Ahmed's consciousness, revealing truths that no language could hold: Earth, they said, is a nexus, a crossroads of probability streams where higher states of existence are accessible to those who dare to see beyond the surface.

He felt engulfed in the vast ocean of consciousness—an all-encompassing flux where time was no longer a relentless river but a liquid domain of infinite possibility, rippling with potentialities. They explained that human beings, especially mystics and visionaries, are natural navigators of these currents; their existence, therefore, is intertwined with the fabric of the infinite. Dimensions beyond physical space unfurled for Ahmed's mind—civilizations of perpetual becoming, where beings had long transcended biological form, existing as pure awareness. Earth's multiple probability paths shimmered like flames in the darkness: one leading toward enlightenment and cosmic mastery, another toward self-destruction, immobilized by fear of the unknown. The beings' message was unambiguous—everyone had a role to play, and the awakening, the recognition of the nexus points, was essential to steer humanity toward its true destiny.

In the final moments of his awakening, Ahmed perceived that consciousness itself was the universe's primal act—its seed and its fruit. Thought, he learned, did not merely reflect reality; it shaped it, unfolding its myriad layers through the act of recognition. The highest heroes, the mystics, the enemies—each embodied different frequencies of that creative force, oscillating on varying continuums of awareness. As he gasped back into his physical form, the scene dissolved into silence, leaving only the memory—and a strange, crystalline object in his hand that hums softly with the energy of the unseen currents. The entire landscape had returned to its familiar visage, yet everything felt altered: the boundaries between worlds had blurred, and Ahmed knew he had crossed a threshold from which no return was quite the same. The ridge of his understanding was forever shifted, the unseen tapestry woven now into the fabric of his mind, ready to guide him toward the next chapter of his unseen voyage, where the line between past, present, and future was forever in flux.

***

Two

The Broken Compass

Displacement and the Search for Truth

The air in the grand hall was thick with the weight of unspoken assertions and the dull clatter of dissenting voices. Scholars, cloaked in their meticulously pressed robes, debated fiercely over Ahmed's latest findings—an interdisciplinary excavation that dared to treat history not merely as a series of narrations but as a tapestry woven with unseen threads of consciousness and perception. His colleagues, many of whom had long anchored their careers within the safe confines of traditional narrative, regarded his propositions with a mixture of condescension and cold suspicion. It was as if his ideas threatened the very foundation of their scholarly domain, unsettling the perceived sanctity of linear chronology, forcing a collective retreat into silence behind the pages of their manuscripts. Yet, beneath the veneer of calm professionalism, Ahmed felt the subtle ripple of something more profound—the simmering friction of truths that refused to be muted, even as the room clamored in denial.

The rejection was swift and dismissive, seasoned with polite but patronizing smiles that masked a growing animosity. His presentation, once delivered with careful authority, now hung in the air like an unfinished symphony—a discordant melody ignored or misunderstood. His assertions about Lawrence's campaigns, intertwined with theories of collective consciousness and temporal distortions, challenged more than just the academic status quo; they brushed against the very fabric of accepted history, unsettling the notions of objectivity and mere recorded fact. Still, as he looked into the eyes of his critics—those hardened by years of academic tradition—Ahmed sensed the faint glow of their silent resistance. Behind their veiled skepticism, he knew a quiet discourse was unfolding—one that refused to be entirely silenced. The classically trained minds clung to the comfort of their predefined narratives, yet within their silent rebuttal, the whispers of a vastly deeper truth persisted, clandestine and waiting to surface.

In the moment between their rejection and the mounting tension, Ahmed's mind drifted to the unspoken currents beneath the visible surface of history—a realm he had begun to perceive as more than mere chronology. It was as if his research had opened a crack in the dense wall of scholarly convention, revealing shadows—partial glimpses—of an existence beyond linear time. The room's lighting seemed to falter at times, as if the very atmosphere itself resisted the confrontation. Whispers of suppressed curiosity echoed softly in the corners, most notably in the suppressed glances exchanged among a few younger colleagues—those whose eyes betrayed a flicker of understanding, a recognition that something fundamental was at stake. On the surface, the meeting disintegrated into sterile formalities, but beneath, a silent struggle unfolded—a contest of truths that dared to breach the boundaries of conventional thought. It was the kind of dispute that lingered on the edges of perception, compelling Ahmed to wonder whether the real conversation was happening behind closed doors, behind their eyes, in the depths where words could not reach.

Later that evening, walking away from the sterile glow of the conference hall into the quiet dusk of Dorset, Ahmed felt an uneasiness grow within him—a feeling that his research had touched upon a hidden chord, one that resonated far beyond the sterile corridors of academia. The landscape softened into an almost mythical expanse—rolling hills cloaked in mist, ancient oaks whispering secrets in a language older than words. It was as though the very earth beneath his feet was echoing with silent truths, waiting for the right moment to surface. The rejection had been expected, yet he sensed an underlying message—an invitation to listen more deeply, to observe what the pages concealed rather than what they explicitly revealed. As the shadows lengthened, he whispered a silent prayer for patience—a recognition that the real dispute was not merely academic, but a cosmic dialogue that transcended language and time itself. Somewhere in this vast and quiet landscape, beneath the silent layers of history and myth, lay a truth that refused to be silenced, waiting for those willing to listen beneath the pages, behind the words.

***

The window of the ruined bungalow, fractured with age yet vibrant with an almost imperceptible glow, cast long shadows that danced on weathered wooden floors worn smooth by decades of silence. Ahmed stepped carefully across the creaking planks, each step echoing softly like a heartbeat from a distant past. Every crack in the plaster, every faded inscription on the walls, seemed imbued with whispers of stories long forgotten—stories carved into the fabric of the building itself, waiting to be rediscovered, reinterpreted. His fingertips traced symbols etched into the woodwork, symbols that felt less like mere decoration and more like an unspoken language bridging worlds both seen and unseen. The air hung thick with the scent of ancient dust and a faint, electrically charged undertone, as though the very ground beneath him pulsed with memories of lost worlds.

In that moment, Ahmed felt the weight of his heritage pressing inward—a burden and a gift alloyed into the marrow of his being. His reflection, fractured by the tarnished glass of a nearby mirror, fractured further by the fissures in his understanding. More than a scholar, more than a man of facts and rational inquiry, he sensed the echoes of a lineage intertwined with the very forces that beckoned him now. The carved calligraphy on the walls—words in Arabic, Persian, and a strange, archaic tongue—resonated with a deeper truth, whispering of ancestors who had navigated these currents long before history's account could record. His own displacement, the dissonance of cultural roots severed and reattached through scholarly pursuit, suddenly appeared acutely shallow, a superficial layer masking an indelible core—a core that the ruins beckoned him to confront.

In the dim glow of the interior, Edith Carrington's voice softly unfurled in his mind—a voice seasoned with the gravity of experience and the calm authority of one who had long dwelled in the spaces between time. She spoke of Lawrence, of the man's restless quest beneath the veneer of adventure, hinting at depths uncharted by conventional history. Her stories painted vivid scenes: Lawrence pacing the fireside in the retreat, reciting verses from sacred texts in the language of the desert, Siegfried Sassoon quietly scribbling notes in an old leather-bound journal, Augustus John's brush captures the flickering shadows as the night deepened. Edith's words wove a narrative far beyond dossiers and battlefield recounts—one that hinted at a truth veiled within the fabric of time itself, a truth that beckoned beyond the reach of rational comprehension. The very landscape, she insisted, was a living archive, inscribed with symbols and currents that only those attuned could decipher.

Her revelations, delivered with the soothing cadence of a guardian of secrets, began to dissolve the boundaries of Ahmed's skepticism. The journals she produced—unparalleled in their age and authenticity—contained meticulous sketches of craft designs unlike any conventional aircraft, yet profoundly familiar in their foreign sophistication. The detailed annotations, written in Lawrence's peculiar hand, described chronological displacements—events where time seemed to warp and bend, where memories and moments flickered with instability. These pages spoke of experiments that transcended military intelligence, venturing into the domain of consciousness and temporality. As Ahmed's eyes devoured every word, he felt a shiver—an awakening that his understanding of history, of self, and of cosmos was no longer bounded by linearity but expanded into a multidimensional dance of possibilities.

Then Edith's voice grew quieter, more insistent, as she revealed that Lawrence's dedication To S.A. was not the simple acknowledgment of a comrade, but an acknowledgment of Sahra Al-Zaman—the Desert of Time—an esoteric portal in the metaphysical landscape. Ahmed visualized the vast, empty sands as a mirror to the mind—an intersection where earth's surface and the currents of eternity converged. Lawrence had, Edith explained, discovered these nodes—points at which the fabric of reality thinned, allowing glimpses into realms beyond ordinary perception. The desert, with its infinite silence, was not merely a physical expanse but a vessel of possibility—a threshold that Lawrence had sought to tap into, to understand, and perhaps, to manipulate. As these thoughts unfurled, Ahmed's rational framework buckled, the pieces of his worldview flickering like a broken mosaic, revealing the jagged yet compelling truth that reality was far more mutable than he had ever believed.

The night deepened, and Edith's tone shifted, rippling with an almost otherworldly timbre. She described her own role as a guardian—selected, long ago, to oversee one of these nexus points—of the pathways where temporal currents intersected. She recounted her childhood, witnessing phenomena that defied explanation: shimmering lights, distortions of sound, glimpses of figures from the past and future coalescing in the periphery of vision. Her stories became visions, her words painting a landscape of beings who existed in dimensions of consciousness far beyond mere matter—entities that communicated not through words but through thought, awareness flowing seamlessly into understanding. Her tone carried a gravity that transcended her age, as if she bore witness to an ongoing saga—one in which humanity was not merely a participant but a key player in a cosmic play of speed, time, and transformation. Ahmed's mind awoke with vividImages of this unseen symphony, a melody playing softly behind the veils of perception.

And then, as if summoned by Edith's revelations, the hour arrived—3:17 AM—what she called Lawrence's hour, a moment not dictated by clock but by cosmic resonance. Outside, the darkness took on an unnatural luminescence. The sky, fractured and shimmering, revealed a craft—indescribably beautiful—oscillating between states of matter and light, capable of shifting into forms that defied the very substance of reality. Its surface rippled like a living membrane, evoking images of liquid mirrors and cosmic metals, as though it existed simultaneously in multiple dimensions. From within this shifting vessel emerged beings of luminous presence—tall, elongated, their forms a suggestion of human evolution unbound by flesh or bone. They radiated a serenity that disturbed the very fabric of human comprehension, as they communicated through what felt like waves of awareness—thoughts, feelings, and visions pouring directly into Ahmed's mind, bypassing language entirely.

These beings explained their purpose with a clarity that resonated beyond formal speech. They were custodians of consciousness, protectors of the thresholds where human awareness fused with the infinite, eternal currents of the cosmos. Their presence, Ahmed realized, was both a revelation and a summons—an invitation to transcend the limitations that dictated linear existence. They revealed that Earth, with all its seeming solidity, was a nexus—a point of convergence where multiple probability streams intersected, each possibility a thread woven into the grand tapestry of the future. Some threads led to humanity's awakening, evolving into beings of luminous consciousness dwelling in realms of pure thought; others spiraled into destruction, oblivious to their own potential or the dangers of the fall into stagnation. Ahmed felt the enormity of this truth settle upon him, a profound awakening that his role was not merely to witness but to carry the torch forward, to become a bridge between worlds, between the seen and the unseen.

His consciousness, now buoyant, drifted through these dimensions—an ascent that felt as light as rebirth, yet as heavy as the weight of eternity. He perceived that these entities, with their eternal gaze, observed Earth's cycles and humanity's choices, defenders of a cosmic balance. Their civilization existed in a state of ongoing becoming, unbound by the restraints of time and space—a state that, in its serenity, shimmered with infinite potential. As they showed him glimpses of Earth's multiple futures—worlds where humans transcend their limitations and worlds where they remain prisoners of their illusions—Ahmed understood the gravity of the task ahead. His duty was clear: to awaken others, to prepare humanity for these thresholds, and to recognize the dormant power within each soul that could turn the tide. The realization sent a shiver through him—a recognition that he was now part of a larger, unfolding story, woven into the eternal dance of consciousness itself.

Then, in the final moments of that celestial encounter, a subtle ripple emanated from the craft, as if ripples of a universe in perpetual motion. Ahmed awoke abruptly, trembling beneath the dawn light filtering through broken windows, alone in the ruins of the forgotten dwelling. Yet, everything had changed. Embedded within his consciousness was a new clarity—a knowledge that defied words but resonated like a chord struck deep within the soul. Beneath layers of dust and debris, he discovered a small crystalline object, warm and humming with energy—an artifact left behind by those beings, as a silent witness and a reminder of the truths glimpsed through the veil of time. Now, burdened and illuminated, Ahmed understood that his life had shifted from scholar to guardian—an inheritor of a legacy forged in the depths of the desert's silence, a bridge to the eternal currents flowing through space and time. As the sun rose higher, casting a pale gold over the landscape, he felt the weight of destiny settle on his shoulders—an unspoken promise to seek beyond the horizon of perceived reality and to carry the unseen torch forward into a future yet undefined, yet undeniably imminent.

***

As Ahmed's battered car coughed its last breath amidst the whispering heather and gnarled yew trees, a strange hush settled over the bleak heathland. The dying light of dusk cast long, ghostly shadows that elongated and intertwined like the threads of a forgotten loom. The landscape, seemingly ordinary in its unassuming austerity, whispered beneath its surface—silent, waiting. The breeze carried a faint metallic scent, unsettling in its subtle reminder that this land held more than mere earth and stone; it harbored secrets that refused to speak but lingered in the air, thick with the unspoken. Ahmed stepped out, his senses prickling, instinct stirring that this was no typical roadside breakdown but a threshold—an invitation into an unseen theatre of the hidden.

He paused, eyes scanning the dimming horizon where the silhouette of Clouds Hill—the legendary refuge of Lawrence—loomed unseen yet present in his mind's eye. The supposed cottage, now lost in twilight, was a mythic symbol to many, but to Ahmed, it was a doorway—an anchor point in a landscape riddled with ambiguities. His gaze was drawn across the uneven terrain, where tufts of grass swayed like silent sentinels. He could feel the land's ancient pulse beneath his feet, a rhythm that transcended the spoken word. Somewhere close, behind a cluster of mossy boulders, an irregular hum vibrated just beneath the sensation of calm, as if the earth itself was flickering with the faint echo of otherworldly activity—an ink-stain upon the fabric of reality that refused to fade. The landscape, modest in size yet monumental in its secrets, seemed to guard its mysteries fiercely, whispering in a language only the initiated could sense.

Drawn by an intangible force, Ahmed found himself wandering toward an unassuming thicket of rhododendrons and silver birch, their shadows woven into the dying amber of the setting sun. Among their tangled branches, an outline emerged—an edifice that, despite its modest façade, radiated a presence beyond mere architecture. Its curved walls and modest dormer windows hinted at a history predating even Lawrence's retreat—a sprawling bungalow concealed by overgrowth, yet subtly commanding in its silence. Warm, golden light spilled from the windows, flickering softly as if alive with unseen vitality. On the veranda, an elegant figure sat with impeccable composure—her posture regal, her gaze piercing yet serene. She was the embodiment of aristocratic dignity made real, as though the land itself had filtered through her veins. With a smile that combined the familiarity of old stories and the distance of forgotten epochs, she extended her hand in greeting, her voice smooth and assured, as if she had summoned him from another time:

"You must be Dr. Ridha. I've been expecting you."

Once inside, the interior transformed his expectations into awe—walls lined with shelves heavy with first editions of Burton's Arabian Nights and Doughty's Arabia Deserta, Persian miniatures whispering tales of lost empires, and silver filigree filling the corners with the gentle shimmer of secrets. The air carried the scent of aged paper, sandalwood, and something darker—perhaps the lingering trace of sacrifice or revelation. Lady Edith Carrington moved with a grace that suggested centuries of cultivation, pouring tea from a delicate porcelain pot into antique cups. The brew was dark, fragrant, and somehow alive—an infusion of silence, history, and memory twisted into each sip. Her stories unfurled like golden thread, weaving tales of Lawrence pacing before fires, reciting Quranic passages in flawless Arabic as Sassoon jotted notes, and Augustus John capturing fleeting gestures on canvas—moments of restless energy that bridged two worlds: the tangible and the ineffable.

She spoke of Lawrence's true nature, beyond the myth—a man haunted by visions of temporal distortions, eager to probe the boundaries of time itself. Her words, laced with knowing, hinted at nights when Lawrence would wander amidst the Dorset hills, apparently chasing whispers—phantoms that defied the logic of linearity. Edith's voice softened as she recounted the late-night debates with Lady Nancy Astor, their discussions stretching into dawn over the future of the Arab world and realms beyond. Her tone darkened slightly when she alluded to the strange phenomena that Lawrence believed he encountered during his solitary rides—phenomena that stirred her own childhood memories of strange lights and whispers in the wind. Each story layered another fragment of Dorset's hidden tapestry—silent, ancient, waiting—urging Ahmed to listen beneath the surface noise of his skepticism.

Then, with deliberate calm, Edith produced a leather-bound volume—Lawrence's missing journals, she claimed, retrieved from a clandestine cache. The handwriting was unmistakably Lawrence's—swift, insistent, alive with fevered insight. Its pages were filled with observations of "chronological displacements"—events that defied conventional explanation, references to "temporal currents," and sketches of craft that shimmered with impossible geometry. Ahmed's heart pounded as he leafed through them, each page dissolving the boundaries he had clung to. The scientific tone of these entries was at odds with traditional military intelligence, hinting at a mission far more profound—an exploration of consciousness, of space and time folding into each other like ribbons in a cosmic dance. The journals revealed that Lawrence had been on the verge of discovering a nexus—a point where the fabric of reality was thin enough to be pierced, where time could be bent and molded by will and awareness.

Lady Edith's voice drew him deeper into the narrative—her words weaving a startling truth behind Lawrence's mysterious dedication "To S.A." She explained that "Sahra Al-Zaman"—the Desert of Time—was not mere poetic symbolism, but a doorway into the depths of the unseen: a ring of Earth where the currents of time intersected, where spiritual and physical realities blurred into one. Lawrence had understood, Edith claimed, that certain locations bore the resistance of this flux—sites where energy and consciousness converged, offering glimpses into other states of existence. Dorset's barren charm, with its silent open spaces, was one such place. And Lawrence's retreat into Clouds Hill was part of a larger, hidden purpose—an attempt to commune with the unseen forces that hovered on the edges of perception. His quest was no longer solely about military victory or political strategy but a search for the eternal—a voyage into the very essence of time and being.

The night air thickened, and Edith's tone grew more hushed, revealing her role as a guardian of one of these nexus points—an eternal watcher committed to preserving the gateways that linked worlds. She described beings that existed beyond ordinary perception—luminous entities, timeless living currents that communicated through thought rather than words. Their presence, she explained, was a whisper on the wind, a flicker in the shadows—a consciousness extending into layers of space that humans conventionally ignore. These entities, she said, had observed Earth's unfolding, guiding certain individuals—Lawrence among them—who harbored the rare gift to see beyond the veil. Their purpose, she affirmed, was to facilitate Earth's transition through a critical thresh-old—a juncture in the evolution of consciousness that demanded recognition of the infinite within the finite. Something shifted in the room, an electric hum that had been absent giving way to a profound stillness—like the opening of a door unseen but felt in every fiber of the body.

Suddenly, a harmonic resonance swelled—not heard with ears but perceived within the mind—drawing Ahmed outside beneath the slowly darkening sky. The landscape around Clouds Hill seemed to ripple, the fabric of reality curling and unfurling at once. The clouds above fractured, revealing a tapestry of shifting light and shadow—an impossible vessel shimmering between dimensions: a craft cloaked in liquid metal, rippling with otherworldly hues, its surface flickering between states of matter as if it defied mere physics. From the craft descended figures that transcended form—tall, luminous, almost ageless—beings whose appearances suggested evolution beyond biological constraints. Their presence was not command but invitation, a gentle but insistent call to transcend ordinary perception and step into the vast ocean of consciousness beyond linear time. They communicated directly—not through words but through the direct flow of thought—filling Ahmed's mind with visions and truths that defied verbal translation. They explained that Earth was approaching a point of divergence, a moment where humanity could awaken to its full potential or be lost in the chaos of ignorance. These guardians, these custodians, had been waiting for an individual like Lawrence—an agent who could act as bridge and interpreter—someone who had gazed into the abyss and returned with a fragment of the infinite.

Ahmed's senses stretched into the infinite space of awareness—a corridor leading beyond the known universe. In this state, he witnessed Earth's multiple probability streams: futures where human consciousness expanded into cosmic realms, and darker outcomes driven by neglect and fear. The guardians revealed that time, far from being a simple river, was a vast liquid ocean—currents of possibility, ripples of potentiality. The ancient beings explained that the key lay not solely in external discovery but within the awakening of innate consciousness—a truth Lawrence understood, buried beneath layers of myth and history. As he floated amid these luminous entities, Ahmed sensed his own consciousness dissolving into a boundless expanse, a place where thought shaped reality—where every intention, every recognition of the divine, could carve new pathways through the fabric of existence. The experience was a paradox: a journey beyond space and time, yet also an immersion into the deepest core of being, where the only certainty was the infinite potential of the mind to become its own universe.

Awaking with a start, Ahmed found himself alone—standing amidst the ruins of the cottage, the morning light bleeding through cracked walls and broken windows. Yet, this was no ordinary dawn; beneath layers of dust and decay, he glimpsed something extraordinary—Lawrence's own manuscripts, maps, and photographs, scattered like remnants of a cosmic puzzle. One map bore markings of temporal anomalies, strange energy points inscribed with meticulous care; another displayed sketches of craft and beings that matched those glimpsed in his vision. His eyes fixated on a leather-bound journal—Lawrence's final notes—written in hurried Arabic script:

Find Sahra Al-Zaman

A sense of urgency seized him, an awareness that he now carried the weight of a mission larger than history or myth. Hidden within a dusty wardrobe, he discovered Lawrence's personal effects—his military coat, Bedouin robes, and a collection of photographs depicting strange figures, some with luminous auras, all bearing an eerie resemblance to the entities he had seen last night.

As dawn broke fully, Ahmed approached the garden, where the legendary Brough Superior sat gleaming, as though awaiting its rider. Though the motorcycle's brass fixtures caught the sunlight, he sensed an unspoken message—an invitation or perhaps a summons. An indistinct figure in leather leathers and goggles appeared, racing across the field with an urgency that pierced his core. The figure, helmeted, obscured, yet somehow familiar, seemed caught in a chase—an inevitable pursuit across dimensions that blurred the boundaries of space and time itself. The moment stretched thin, an echo in eternity where the known fractured into fragments of possibility. Just as the figure disappeared beyond the horizon, everything around him dissolved into the same silent, secret landscape that had beckoned him since the beginning. The fragile ruins, the cryptic artifacts—they all whispered of a truth that permeated beyond his understanding, hinting at a vast cosmic narrative where he had become a participant rather than an observer. Standing amidst the awakening landscape, Ahmed sensed that the mysteries of Dorset's diminutive domain were only just beginning to reveal their true scope—a landscape not just of land but of consciousness, and perhaps, of salvation.

***

Three

Bovington Heath at Dusk

Crossing the Threshold

The engine's sudden cessation cut through the fading light with brutal suddenness, leaving Ahmed's car stranded amidst the dense thicket of rhododendrons and ancient birch, their skeletal branches whispering secrets on the evening breeze. The metallic splinter of the breakdown resonated unnaturally, as if the very mechanism that once responded to human command had betrayed him, turning silent at the threshold of something unknowable. The distant hum of the motor—the familiar pulse of rationality—disappeared into an eerie hush, leaving a residue of unease that clung to the air like fog on the heath. Shadows lengthened quickly, stretching toward him with a deliberate patience, as though the landscape itself conspired to cast him adrift into a different sphere of existence.

Ahmed sat behind the steering wheel, ears straining for any flicker of mechanical life, but nothing stirred. His mind raced, flickering between frustration and suspicion, deciding whether this failure was mere coincidence or an initial sign of that which lurked beyond his grasp. The landscape around him seemed imbued with a strange stillness—trees blackened silhouettes against a violet dusk that deepened with each passing moment. A faint, almost imperceptible hum vibrated through the air, not mechanical but something more subtle, woven into the fabric of the twilight. It was as if the earth beneath him had paused, waiting, and his small car became a mere point on a vast, inscrutable map of shifting realities.

Drawing a deep breath, Ahmed flicked open the door, the gravel crunching softly beneath his feet. The silence pressed against him, a weight of expectation unspoken but palpably present. As he moved toward the trunk to retrieve his flashlight, a fleeting flicker of sensation passed through him—an inexplicable prickling at the nape of his neck, reminding him that the boundary he approached was no ordinary mechanical or physical barrier. With cautious resolve, he walked toward the driver's side window, gazing out into the gathering gloom, where the boundary between science and something far more elusive seemed to blur with every heartbeat. The landscape was silent, but its silence pulsed with the promise of revelations beyond the known, at the very edge where mystery and mechanics intertwined.

His fingers hovered over the latch, hesitating beneath the weight of anticipation. The moment the door swung open, a shiver ran through him—not from cold but from an inward acknowledgment that the failure of the engine was not accidental. It marked a crossing into an uncharted territory—a rupture in the fabric of linear causality. Outside, the twilight dissolved into a strange liminal space; the sky cracked apart like fragile parchment, revealing seams of shimmering light that flickered unpredictably. The landscape stretched into other dimensions, each one whispering fragments of histories yet to be written or faded from collective memory. Ahmed's eyes flicked across the horizon, sensing that this mechanical failure was perhaps the least of what lay just beyond his sight—a sign of larger forces at work on the threshold of perception.

Suddenly, a faint resonance seemed to hum from the shadows, a vibration that sealed the divide between the material and the spectral. The landscape itself felt alive—layers of time and space folding inward—to reveal hints of a realm where physics bowed and obeyed no laws but rather the subtle dictates of consciousness. The air thickened, imbued with an electric charge, as if reality itself was trembling on the verge of opening a portal. Ahmed felt his heartbeat quicken, a visceral awareness that the boundary he faced was a gateway. His rational mind struggled to grasp the sensation—was this failure of machinery merely coincidental, or an opening carved by unseen forces working in tandem with the currents of the mysterious horizon?

In the breathless pause that followed, the boundary flickered—light bending bizarrely, shadows dancing in perpetual flux—signaling that he was standing at the nexus of worlds, on the edge of something both ancient and unknown. His eyes fixated on the fractured sky, where the heavens seemed to ripple like water disturbed by an unseen hand. He knew, unshakably, that beyond this rupture lay the possibility of uncovering truths that would redefine every certitude he had ever held. The landscape's silence was active, pregnant with potential, whispering in spectral languages of what might be available—hidden in the dimming dusk—to anyone daring enough, or perhaps destined, to step beyond the mechanical collapse into the vast mystery that beckoned.

***

The air grew thicker as Ahmed's car ground to an abrupt halt amidst the heather and silver birches that lined the winding Dorset road. Dusk cast long, trembling shadows over Bovington Heath, its quiet solemnity disturbed only by the occasional distant cry of a hunting owl or the shuffling of unseen creatures in the underbrush. The engine's dying rasp seemed to echo the fading light—an ominous sign, almost prophetic—portending a crossing into something unspoken, something beyond ordinary comprehension. Ahmed stepped out into the chilly evening, feeling the weight of the landscape pressing against his skin, as if the land itself whispered secrets just beyond the threshold of his understanding.

He looked up toward Clouds Hill, which loomed on the horizon like a sentinel guarding the border between worlds. The sky, already darkening into slate-gray shades, fractured in places as if the fabric of reality itself was beginning to tremble. The hill seemed to breathe, its silhouette shifting subtly—the topography alive with an anticipation that defied the rational mind. For a moment, Ahmed hesitated, his gaze drawn to the faint glow emanating from the distant cottage. It was unlike any ordinary light; it pulsed gently, harmonizing with the pounding of his heart, attuning him to an unspoken consciousness that beckoned him closer, as if the myth of Clouds Hill was on the verge of transforming into something startlingly real.

As he approached, the pathway beneath his feet seemed to ripple softly—a delicate oscillation that set his senses on edge. The landscape, with its tangled thickets and mossed stones, hinted at stories buried deep within its shadows. The very air felt charged, thick with fragments of memories long suppressed—images of Lawrence pacing, reciting, dreaming. When he finally crossed the boundary that separated the open heath from the grounds of the old cottage, the gentle hum of unseen currents grew insistent. Reality was beginning to blur, the myth of Clouds Hill slipping dangerously close—no longer a distant legend but a threshold pierced by whispers of the impossible.

Bright, warm light spilled from the cottage's windows, promising refuge—or perhaps revelation. Ahmed hesitated only a moment before stepping onto the covered veranda, where an elderly woman sat elegantly in a carved wooden chair. Her bearing was aristocratic, her movements precise yet effortless—a presence that seemed rooted in centuries of history. Eyes like dark pools of ink regarded him quietly, as if she had been expecting him all along. She rose, with a grace that defied her age, and extended a delicate hand.

"You've come far, dear visitor," she said softly, her voice a melody that seemed to resonate directly with his core. "It's time you saw what lies beyond the stories—a place where myth and reality intertwine, and the line between worlds is disturbingly thin."

The interior astonished him, a sanctuary of contradiction—walls lined with first editions of Burton's Arabian Nights and Doughty's Arabia Deserta, Persian miniatures shimmering beneath layers of age and history, Bedouin silver glinting like captured moonlight. The air was fragrant with cardamom and aged paper, an intoxicating blend of culture and memory. On a sturdy oak table, a tray of rare Pu-erh tea awaited, its aroma deep and earthy, as if steeped in centuries of clandestine knowledge. Lady Edith Carrington poured with a practiced hand, her movements deliberate, as if she moved through dimensions as easily as through space. She sipped thoughtfully, then fixed her gaze on Ahmed, her eyes luminous with an inner fire.

"This place is more than a refuge," she murmured. "It's a threshold, a nexus, a conduit for truths hidden just beneath the surface of history and myth."

She spoke of gatherings—intimate circles where Lawrence, Sassoon, and others had met in clandestine exchange, their voices weaving stories that sounded woven from moonlight and old stone. Lawrence, she claimed, was never merely the soldier or the adventurer, but a seeker who watched the boundaries of time itself. By night, he would pace these rooms, reciting passages from the Quran with perfect Arabic, while Sassoon scribbled in notebooks and Augustus John sketched the restless expressions on Lawrence's face. Yet, Edith's words grew more enigmatic, hinting that Lawrence's retreat to this cottage was less about withdrawal and more about investigation—an exploration of burgeoning anomalies that teased at the fabric of linear time. She told of her own childhood memories, of strange phenomena she had witnessed, the sky shimmering with patterns no scientific instrument could explain, her awareness extending beyond the limits of conventional understanding.

Then she produced Lawrence's journals—authentic, she insisted, their pages filled with handwriting that shimmered with a life of its own, unbound by the typical confines of historical documentation. Here, in the flickering candlelight, Ahmed glimpsed detailed accounts that read more like scientific notes: observations of what he recognized as "chronological displacement events," theories on consciousness transcending the flow of time, sketches of craft astonishing in their unfamiliarity—machines that defied the known laws of aerodynamics, yet bore the unmistakable mark of Lawrence's hand. As these pages turned under Edith's guiding fingers, Ahmed began to sense that the legend wasn't simply about military campaigns or political upheaval, but about an ancient, ongoing investigation into the very nature of reality.

Most profoundly, Edith deciphered the cryptic significance of the dedication "To S.A." in Seven Pillars of Wisdom, revealing it as an homage to "Sahra Al-Zaman"—the Desert of Time—a concept Lawrence stumbled upon in his secret studies. It was not merely a poetic image, but a black hole of sorts—a metaphysical crossroads where locations across Earth condensed into zones of intense temporal flux. The desert, she explained softly, was a place where the boundaries of past, present, and future dissolved into a single moment—a place where Lawrence believed humanity could access higher states of consciousness if only it knew how to decipher its signals. To Edith, these "points" created invisible threads in the fabric of reality, links that, once understood, could lead humans across the thresholds of time itself.

The night deepened into a profound silence, broken only by Edith's whispered stories of beings—luminescent entities that guard the nexus points from the unseen, their presence hinted at in dreams and fleeting visions. She painted pictures of Lawrence's last days here, hinting at an esoteric mission that reached far beyond the Arab Revolt, extending into territories that no history could record. As her words floated in the air, Ahmed felt his rational mind trembling, the boundaries of scientific skepticism slowly dissolving like ice in a warm current. His skin prickled with the electric charge of anticipation, the line between myth and reality wavering dangerously as he sensed he was on the cusp of witnessing something that transcended history—a doorway into the infinite.

Suddenly, at exactly 3:17 AM—what Edith called "Lawrence's hour"—a soft harmonic resonance stirred the air, vibrating through his bones, whispering of gateways beyond space and time. Drawn by an irresistible force, he stepped out into the garden, leaves shimmering as if they carried their own secret frequencies. Above Clouds Hill, the sky fractured in a cascade of shifting light, revealing a craft of impossible complexity—its surface a kaleidoscope of polished metal, liquid light, and textures beyond any natural form. The surface seemed to pulse, shifting seamlessly between states, as if the boundaries of matter were merely illusions. Aurora-like streaks danced along its contours, hinting at an intelligence that stretched across dimensions—a realm where shape and substance dissolved into pure energy.

From the craft emerged beings, their forms gliding into the field of view—not as humans or animals, but as luminous entities of raw consciousness. Tall and shimmering, their silhouettes shimmered with evolution's unseen hand, their eyes glowing with understanding and patience.

Without words, they communicated through waves of thought—images, feelings, impressions—flowing directly into Ahmed's mind. Their message was clear: they were custodians of consciousness, guides for those who could access the threshold. They explained that Earth itself was a constantly shifting nexus of potential futures, some luminous and others shadowed in ruin; that Lawrence's work was a part of a larger effort to guide humanity through this cosmic crossroads.

The experience smothered his rational defenses, sweeping him into a realm of pure awareness, where the boundaries of self dissolved into the universal ocean. They revealed that consciousness, not matter, was the foundation of all existence—a living fabric woven from intention and perception. Time, they said, was a liquid, not a river—a vast ocean of possibilities rippling with currents only perceptible beyond linear sense. These beings—beings that had long transcended form—offered a vision of civilization in continuous evolution, a perpetual becoming that crowned the universe with layers of higher consciousness. Ahmed's entire perception shifted, understood suddenly that the man he once was merely peered at the surface of such depths, glimpsing only a fraction of what could be attained.

Awakening from this vision, he found himself alone amid the ruins, yet everything had subtly transformed. Excavating beneath the debris, he uncovered a hidden archive—walls lined with correspondence from Lawrence, Sassoon, and others, along with maps dotted with strange symbols denoting temporal anomalies. Lawrence's own typewriter, an Underwood No. 5, still gleamed faintly under a layer of dust, resting on a weathered desk. On the sheet of paper inserted, he now saw a single phrase—and it was in Lawrence's flowing Arabic script: "Find Sahra Al-Zaman," the Desert of Time, a cipher and a key all in one. The message resonated with a new significance: Lawrence's true mission was not only political or military but aimed at awakening that part of humanity capable of navigating the labyrinth of time. It was a map written in symbols—a call to those who could sense the subtle whispers of the threshold and heed their summons.

In the wardrobe, untouched by decay, he discovered Lawrence's personal effects: the familiar leather-bound maps, Bedouin robes, and the motorcycle—the Brough Superior SS100—gleaming as if newly restored, its brass fittings catching the faint dawn light as if poised for one final ride. Yet, what haunted him most was the discovery of recent entries—reminiscent of handwriting, yet somehow more urgent, more alive—notes that spoke of encounters with strange creatures, beings that seemed to exist outside of time itself. Then he saw it: a small crystalline device, tucked within a drawer, shimmering with an inner light that pulsed softly. Its purpose was unknown, but its presence confirmed that the boundary between science and myth was now irrevocably breached. The legacy was clear: Lawrence had been a guardian—a seeker—who glimpsed the infinite and sought to prepare others to do the same.

As the first streaks of sunlight pierced the horizon, Ahmed looked back toward the cottage's ruin, and in doing so, understood that the myth of Clouds Hill had not merely been a quaint history or a heroic legend, but a living portal—an open door to higher states of awareness. Every fragment of the landscape, every artifact, had become part of a vast, unspoken story unfolding beyond time's linear confines, waiting for those willing to listen. He realized his journey had only just begun; now, with the consciousness unlocked, he carried not only the weight of memories but the responsibility of guiding humanity toward the cosmic threshold—and ensuring that the myth, once on the verge of fading into legend, would become a living, breathing reality.

***

The dusk settled slowly over Bovington Heath, casting elongated shadows that stretched like fingers across the heather and gorse, wrapping the landscape in a quiet, contemplative hush. The air grew dense with the scent of damp earth and ancient wood, as if time itself had paused, holding its breath in anticipation. It was in this liminal space—between fading daylight and encroaching night—that Lady Edith Carrington made her appearance, her figure emerging from the shadows with an effortless dignity that seemed both deliberate and timeless. She moved with a measured grace, a silent assertion that she belonged to a realm just beyond the ordinary, a whisper between worlds. Her presence seemed to ripple through the stagnant stillness, unsettling the very fabric of the fading evening as though she carried with her a secret that refused to stay buried in the past.

Her entrance was not marked by fanfare or a sudden flare of light, but rather by the subtle shift in atmosphere—a gentle bringing forth of the extraordinary from the mundane. As if summoned by unseen currents, her figure appeared on the veranda of an old bungalow almost lost among the persistent rhododendrons and silver birch trees that swayed softly, whispering their own stories to the coming night. She paused at the threshold, her gaze sweeping over the landscape with a serenity that belied a profound awareness. Her eyes, sharp yet softened by time, seemed to hold the depths of countless histories—stories that bridged epochs and consciousness alike. The light from within spilled onto her silhouette, casting her as a guardian between the shadowed world she inhabited and the one awakening beyond her gentle facade.

Her arrival felt like a brushstroke on a canvas stretched between myth and memory. With measured deliberation, she ascended the stone steps, her movements embodying the fluidity of a dance learned long ago, before the boundaries of linear time had become rigid. She seemed not to step into the present but to glide into it, as though she had slipped through a fabric woven from threads of the past, present, and something yet to be known. Her figure, illuminated by the warm glow of oil lamps and flickering candles, projected an aura of quiet authority—yet it was a grace that beckoned, an invitation to cross into a space where history and the unseen converged. Ahmed, watching from a distance, felt an inexplicable pull—his rational mind struggling to grasp the reality unfolding before him. Yet, beneath his skepticism, a faint tremor of recognition stirred, an instinct that this was no ordinary moment—a threshold about to be crossed by someone who had mastered the delicate art of existence between worlds.

Grace, in her essence, was her language—an unspoken dialogue with the universe, a silent understanding so profound that words seemed inadequate to capture its depth. Her posture reflected a life lived beyond ordinary constraints, bearing the imprint of aristocratic refinement and a mysterious intimacy with the wider currents of time. As she stepped forward without haste, her face became a luminous canvas—eyes shimmering with stories, perhaps of lovers long departed, or secrets kept from the ages. Her lips curved with a faint smile that was both reassuring and enigmatic, hinting at a knowledge that bridged the corporeal and the divine. In that moment, she became a living embodiment of grace between worlds—a vessel through which the ancient powers, the whispering currents, could flow into the present, inviting those who dared to see beyond the surface into the depths of eternity.

Ahmed's breath caught as her presence seemed to dissolve the boundaries he had meticulously constructed around his worldview. Her very existence challenged the notion that reality was bound by time's relentless march or the linear constraints of cause and effect. Instead, she radiated a quiet authority—a delicate yet unwavering authority—that suggested she was both witness and guardian of a realm where history, myth, and consciousness intertwined like the strands of a clandestine loom. Her step was neither hurried nor rigid, but imbued with the calm assurance of one who had traversed many thresholds and returned with stories from the shadowed edges of human understanding. Each movement spoke of a balance between the seen and the unseen, a harmony that beckoned

Ahmed toward an aperture of possibility he had long dismissed as mere fantasy. Yet, as her figure grew clearer, so too did the realization that she carried within her an awareness that might rewrite the very fabric of his quest, and perhaps, of humanity's destiny itself.

Her entrance, subtle yet transformative, marked not just the beginning of a meeting but a crossing—an opening into that space where time's illusion unraveled and the eternal whispered through the cracks of the ordinary world. The silence that surrounded her grew laden with meaning, as if the landscape itself leaned in to listen. Ahmed felt a tremor deep within, a realization that the woman before him was a conduit—a living bridge between the mortal and the infinite. Her grace was not merely physical but spectral, an elegant affirmation that the journey he had begun was no longer confined to scholarly pursuits but had become a venture into the very core of existence. As she finally stepped onto the veranda, her every movement seemed to say that the threshold had been breached, and what lay beyond was a domain where history and eternity converged—a realm awaiting those bold enough to enter without fear.

***

Four
The Hidden Bungalow

Architecture of Memory and Time

The bungalow rose from the bosom of the Dorset heath with an unassuming grace, its woodwork intricately carved with motifs that seemed almost alive—twisting vines, abstract figures, interlaced patterns that shimmered faintly in the dying light. Its windows held a cloudy sheen, as if layers of stained glass had been compressed into translucent panels, distorting the flickering firelight within into glimmers of color and shadow that played tricks on the eye. The architecture, rooted deeply in Arts and Crafts tradition, was more than mere aesthetics; it carried a silent language of symbols and omens, as if deliberately concealing gateways to regions beyond ordinary perception. Ahmed, standing on the threshold under the weight of a dusk that thickened into an ink of impending night, felt the faint pulse of something unseen beneath the surface—an anomaly woven into the very fabric of its design, beckoning or warning, he could not yet tell.

Inside, the air was thick with an unplaceable scent—aged paper, faint cinnamon, the subtle aroma of incantations or memories long encoded in the walls. Shelves bowed under the weight of books—first editions of Burton's Arabian Nights interlaced with Doughty's Arabia Deserta, Persian miniatures shimmering behind glass, and objects of silver and lapis lazuli that seemed to hum with a quiet energy, resonant with their own stories. Every surface appeared curated not just for beauty, but as a ledger of human consciousness caught in transit—artifacts that spoke softly of histories layered upon each other like sediment. The walls, lined with correspondence from luminaries of the early twentieth century—Sassoon, Lawrence, even silent letters of generals long dead—formed a mosaic of whispered echoes. These objects, these tiny worlds of detail, served as keys—or perhaps signs—pointing to a hidden realm veiled behind the apparent humdrum of a rustic dwelling. Ahmed's fingers brushed the ornate carvings, sensing a language of geometry and cryptic symbolism, as if the very design refused to be read at face value, demanding instead an intuitive deciphering rooted in ancient craft and unseen knowledge.

As Lady Edith poured the rich, dark pu-erh into delicate porcelain cups, her manner revealed a seasoned confidence, a queenly grace that neither dismissed nor overly emphasized the stakes at hand. She spoke softly, her voice a gentle cadence that seemed to ripple through the room, bridging the material and the metaphysical. Her stories extricated Ahmed from his scientific skepticism; she recounted nights when Lawrence would pace before the fireplace, reciting interpolated passages from the Quran in a voice that still lingered in her memory—precise, ritualistic, as if summoning something beyond words. Sassoon scribbled notes—a rare glimpse of the poet's quiet rebellion—and Augustus John sketched luminous, restless figures, caught forever in a moment of suspended motion. Edith's anecdotes painted a picture of Lawrence not as a mere soldier or scholar but as a seeker whose restless mind constantly probed the boundaries of perception. Her words suggested that his retreat to Clouds Hill was more than strategic withdrawal; it was an investigation into a phenomena that defied comprehension—a convergence of linear and non-linear currents twisting through Dorset's quiet landscape.

The moment shifted when Edith produced Lawrence's journals, their aged leather covers crackling softly under her careful handling. The pages, filled with dense, meticulous handwriting, were unmistakably authentic—no replica, no forgery. They contained detailed observations that read more like scientific reports than military notes: numbered entries on "chronological displacement events," diagrams of strange craft, and theoretical musings on consciousness as a variable capable of transcending time's relentless march. Lawrence's words chronicled experiences of crossing boundaries — moments where past, present, and future blurred into a single point of awareness, where the linear thread of history unraveled into a web of infinite possibilities. In one entry, he described witnessing "a shift in the fabric of time," a ripple felt tangibly during a desert patrol, as if the sands themselves were veins through which eternity pulsed differently. Another sketch depicted a craft—an object that bore no resemblance to earthly technology—its contours shifting between solid and liquid states, as if splattered across dimensions. Ahmed's rational mind frantically sought explanations; the scientific journals within him recognized anomalies, yet the cumulative weight of the journals suggested truths that refused to be confined within ordinary confines of logic.

Then Edith whispered softly, her voice thick with reverence, that Lawrence's inscription "To S.A."—long thought a cryptic dedication—meant "Sahra Al-Zaman," the "Desert of Time," a concept rooted deep in esoteric thought. It was not a metaphor but an active force. To her, the desert had been a fluid conduit, a space where Earth's temporal currents intersected in ways not yet understood. Her words painted an image of barren stretches that conceal gateways—portals to realms precisely at the edge of perception. She spoke of her own role, as a guardian standing at these junctions, watching over the invisible threads that connect one consciousness to another across epochs. Lawrence, she claimed, had been a pioneer of this hidden knowledge—an explorer who glimpsed the malleability of time itself, embedding that insight in his work and his retreat into the Dorset landscape, seeking the truth behind the veils that separate worlds. The room's atmosphere grew heavier with unspoken significance, as if each artifact and each word stitched together a broader, cosmic fabric hiding just beneath the veneer of the ordinary.

In the silence that followed, the verdict of the universe whispered—a hint of things beyond the grasp of science, beyond even history's many narratives. Edith's tone shifted, her voice dropping to a near-whisper, when she described the beings she called "Guardians"—entities that had monitored Earth from unseen currents, higher consciousness incarnate, watching over the unfolding of human awareness. She spoke of her own duty, of luminous, formless intelligences whose existence defied words yet communicated through a language of images and resonances—thoughts transmitted directly into the mind, bypassing speech entirely. It was as if the very fabric of reality was woven from the threads of consciousness, a cosmic loom that these beings kept in balance. As night descended, Ahmed's skepticism dissolved piece by piece; his worldview crumbled beneath the weight of her stories, each one more unearthly and compelling than the last. He sensed that the bungalow's design—its curiously embedded motifs and cryptic symbols—was not accidental but a symbolic map, encoded with the keys to navigation through these shifting realms.

The climax unfolded at precisely 3:17 AM—what Edith called "Lawrence's hour"—an appointed moment when the universe itself seemed to tremble. Outside, the sky beyond the bungalow fractured as if torn from the pages of an ancient manuscript, revealing a procession of shifting shapes and shimmering light. In that moment, the fabric of the cosmos fluttered like gossamer—an opening, not just in space, but within the deepest layers of perception. Ahmed's senses blurred as a harmony of unseen frequencies flooded his consciousness—an infinite symphony of vibrations resonating across dimensions. A craft, impossible to characterize fully—neither matter nor energy, but something other—hovered just above the landscape, its surface flickering between metals and liquids, shimmering like a mirage that refused to fade. Within that shimmering construct, tall luminous figures materialized—beings that radiated intelligence beyond human imagination, their forms evolving seamlessly, embodying a state of consciousness unbound by physical laws. Their mere presence was an act of awakening—an invitation to step beyond the limits of space-time and into a realm where time is not linear but a liquid, malleable substance.

They communicated without words, their thoughts flooding into Ahmed's mind like a rushing tide—images, words, and feelings compressing across languages and epochs. They explained their nature as custodians of awareness, guardians of the thresholds that lay scattered across Earth, sensing the collective evolution of human consciousness. Their message was clear: Earth approached a pivotal junction—the moment where human understanding could leap into higher dimensions or retreat into the darkness of ignorance. Ahmed, overwhelmed yet inexplicably transformed, realized he had crossed into a realm beyond the known—where the craft and the beings shimmered with the fabric of creation itself, echoing Lawrence's deep understanding of the desert's unearthly secrets.

The ocean of probability stretched infinitely before him: worlds where mankind had transcended time, and others where it failed, trapped in the impasse of linear illusion. He saw, vividly and viscerally, that consciousness was the genesis, the ongoing creation of all reality—a force capable of shaping worlds, dissolving barriers, and unlocking secrets kept hidden since the dawn of existence. When dawn finally crested the horizon, the beings vanished as suddenly as they appeared—leaving Ahmed alone, trembling, clutching a crystalline fragment of otherworldly origin. The cottage, once alive with cosmic presence, now stood silent, its walls whispering a final secret: the will to awaken is the only key—one that each soul must turn for the threshold to open.

***

As Ahmed stepped across the threshold of the bungalow, an immediate sense of layered containment enveloped him. The architecture, with its intricate woodwork carved in an artful chaos, seemed alive—threads of history woven through every beam, every panel. The fireplace, enormous and carved from dark stone, bore symbols that blurred in and out of focus, as if whispering secrets only perceptible to a consciousness willing to listen beyond the surface. Light played tricks across the ceiling beams, casting shadows that seemed to pulse gently, suggesting the walls themselves were functioning as part of an unseen mechanism—an interface between worlds. The very arrangement of furniture defied logic, with chairs placed at odd angles, rugs seemingly floating just above the floor, their intricate patterns humming softly with an energy that felt both ancient and restless.

Within this labyrinth of design, Ahmed felt the flicker of something more—a subtle anomaly encoded into every material, every ornament. Persian miniatures, tiny and intensely detailed, seemed to shift in glimpses, revealing fleeting visions of stars and distant landscapes. Bedouin silverware, carefully arranged on shelves, shimmered with an unnatural luminescence, as if reflecting a dimension beyond the visible. Walls lined with correspondence and artifacts from luminaries of the 20th century appeared to resonate with an otherworldly timbre; their ink and engravings humming softly, subtly alive, as if alive with consciousness. The space was a labyrinth of symbols with no clear beginning or end, yet each element seemed deliberately placed to shield deeper layers of understanding—like a coded language hiding secrets that defied linear comprehension.

Lady Edith Carrington's voice interrupted the flow of suspicion and wonder, her tone imbued with the calm authority of someone who had navigated the thresholds of worlds many times. She poured tea—deep, dark pu-erh, its aroma thick and complex—claiming it was a gift from Ned himself. As she gestured for Ahmed to taste, her eyes held the faint glint of knowing, of possessing knowledge carved into her existence like the carvings of her house. Her words danced around the paradoxes of the architecture: how the design's anomalies extended beyond aesthetics, serving as fabric woven from the threads of unseen currents, channels through which time itself might ripple or fold. These architectural quirks, she explained softly, were not accidental but deliberate—manifestations of intentional gateways intended to conceal portals for those capable of perceiving them.

As night deepened, the boundaries between the external world and the internal realm dissolved further. Edith's stories—rich with details of Lawrence pacing before fires and reciting passages in arabesque—began to take on the quality of living memory, alive and inflected with whispers from the past. Her tales suggested that Lawrence's retreat was more than a sanctuary from war; it was a location of critical importance—an anchoring point where the very fabric of time could be glimpsed as malleable. She recounted how Lawrence would often stay awake into the earliest hours, his voice whispering codes and invitations to worlds beyond the mere documents of history. Edith herself had witnessed signs of these anomalies from childhood, fleeting distortions in the landscape, moments when the sky flickered as if a curtain was being lifted just enough to hint at what lay behind it all.

When she produced Lawrence's journals—shrouded in dust but unmistakably authentic—the atmosphere shifted palpably. The pages, fragile yet resilient, were filled with meticulous handwriting and annotations that bore the weight of scientific inquiry rather than mere military strategy. The accounts of chronological displacement events sounded like observations of phenomena that defied common sense—visions of landscapes shifting, figures flickering into and out of existence, and experiments that sought to understand consciousness as a dimension rather than a mere state of mind. The sketches within displayed craft and devices that bore no resemblance to contemporary technology, their forms oscillating between metallic, crystalline, and liquid states, as if existing in a realm of pure potential—a realm governed by principles unknown to physics but familiar to the depths of the mind.

Most magnetic of all was the revelation of the true meaning behind Lawrence's inscrutable dedication To S.A.—not the widely accepted homage, but a clandestine acknowledgment of Sahra Al-Zaman, a profound metaphor for The Desert of Time. Edith explained that Lawrence believed certain sites on Earth were woven into a network of intersecting temporal currents—places where the boundary between present and eternity thinned to nothing. The desert, with its vast emptiness, was the greatest of these gateways—a mirror and a mirror's mirror—where perception could transcend the linearity of history and access higher states of consciousness, if only one knew how to listen. Her words hinted at the ancient wisdom he had uncovered, a knowledge that hinted at layered realities and the very fabric of existence being more fluid and responsive than anyone dared suppose.

As the clock moved beyond midnight, Edith's voice softened into a reverent whisper, revealing her role as caretaker of one such nexus—a guardian of the invisible currents that connect entire dimensions. Her stories told of beings—luminous, elongated forms—that watched silently from beyond the constraints of physics, their purpose to oversee humanity's awakening and evolution. They communicated via energy and thought, not words; their presence, sensed rather than seen, was like the gentle pull of a tide, guiding or warning according to the needs of the moment. She told of Lawrence's clandestine experiments—trials and tribulations in understanding the interactions of consciousness and time—outlays meant not merely to decipher history but to unlock the door to an entirely new realm of perception and being.

Ahmed's rational mind, once a fortress of doubt, began to crumble beneath the weight of these disclosures. His skepticism was tested by the subtle, pervasive sense that he was standing at the cusp of something—an insistent whisper that he was being called to step beyond the limits of conventional understanding. A strange resonance, nearly tactile, vibrated in the air, leading him outside into the night, where the sky above Clouds Hill seemed to fracture like ancient parchment—lines and textures revealing the workings of a universe beyond his senses. What he saw defied explanation: a craft of dazzling beauty, shimmering through multiple dimensions simultaneously. Its surface undulated with the evanescence of light, morphing between states—polished metal, liquid crystal, and sheer, unseeable potential—traversing the boundaries of perception itself.

From this swirling maelstrom emerged beings—tall, luminous, flowing—whose forms stretched and contracted, echoing beyond human limitations. They communicated directly into his mind, their thoughts carrying scripts in multiple languages—Arabic, English, and primeval tongues predating speech—flowing like a river of understanding that washed over him in waves. Their purpose was clear: they were custodians of consciousness evolution, entities that had watched silent generations pass in their ongoing task of guiding the collective emergence into higher awareness. Ahmed understood then that this was no coincidence; these beings had monitored Earth's temporal pathways since long before recorded history, and now, at the precipice of a cosmic transition, he was being invited to join the ongoing procession—no longer as a mere observer but as a participant in the unfolding of a new chapter.

Their civilization existed in a state of fluid becoming, a harmony of existence beyond the constraints of physical form. They revealed to him the multiple probability streams of human destiny—futures shimmering like distant reflections in a placid lake, some radiant with evolutions beyond imagination, others darkened by failure to recognize the true nature of existence. Humanity, they explained, was on the verge of an evolutionary leap, a crossing point where consciousness would either expand into its innate cosmic potential or regress into chaos. The choice, they intimated, was embedded within each individual's awareness—each moment of perception shaping the course of history as it spiraled toward the inevitable threshold, where the fabric of time itself might unravel or be woven anew.

Images flooded his consciousness: a universe not a river rushing forward but an ocean deep and vast, brimming with currents and ripples—paths of possibility that shimmered and intertwined. The beings spoke of mystics and visionaries who navigated these currents intuitively, their minds attuned to the deeper symphony underlying existence. Ahmed sensed that his own awakening was part of this grander design—an arrival at a critical juncture where perception would redefine what it meant to be human. Terrified and exhilarated, he felt the infinite potential awaiting his choosing, a universe of endless facets opened before him like the petals of a cosmic lotus unfolding within his mind.

Awakening, he found himself no longer outside but within a space of pure awareness—an extension into realms where the physical dissolves into thought, where time is no longer a line but a liquid, swirling and shifting beneath his touch. The ruins of the cottage appeared to fade, replaced by a radiant consciousness that responded to his presence. He realized that his journey had transcended mere exploration—it was a calling to act as a bridge, a vessel through which humanity's understanding could expand. The beings' final message echoed as a gentle crescendo—an imperative to recognize the true power innate in thought and consciousness, and the necessity of awakening to these truths before the closing of the cosmic gate. As he drifted back into wakefulness, the last image etched into his mind was the silhouette of a figure racing across the horizon in leather and chrome—a rider chasing a shadow that shimmered just beyond the reach of sight, embodying the relentless pursuit of the infinite that now pulsed within him.

***

Inside the shadowed embrace of the rambling bungalow, the air hung heavy with the scent of aged parchment and lingering incense. Walls lined with layers of faded fabric and tapestries seemed to pulse with secrets, as if whispering fragments of a forgotten time. Ahmed's eyes flicked over the array of objects—an ornate brass compass etched with unfamiliar symbols, a faded photograph of Lawrence in his uniform, and a collection of delicate glass vials filled with liquids golden and dark. Each artifact radiated an unseen charge, hinting at stories far beyond human understanding, stories that could unravel the entire fabric of history itself. The dim, golden glow from the windows flickered in tandem with his racing pulse, casting long, shifting shadows that hinted at truths lying just beyond sight.

Edith's voice, soft yet resonant, cut through the silence as she presented a battered leather-bound journal, its pages spilling with ink-stained notes. This was Lawrence's own handwriting, she murmured, her fingertips tracing the faded letters. The lines displayed observations almost scientific in tone—detailed accounts of momentary disruptions in his campaigns, sudden displacements in time that defied logic. Words like 'dislocation,' 'resonance,' and 'null zones' flashed in Ahmed's mind, stirring a pang of wonder and skepticism. Edith explained that Lawrence believed certain sites on Earth weren't merely geographical points, but nexus points where the fabric of reality was thin—cracks in the infinite, portals to realms of consciousness yet uncharted. Her gentle gaze held a familiarity with the objects that suggested she had long been a keeper of these secrets, entrusted with guarding the very pathways Ahmed now sought to understand. She added, almost whispering, that Lawrence's fascination with these zones extended well beyond empirical curiosity—he sensed a higher purpose, a mission intertwined with the soul of the universe itself.

As the hours deepened, Edith's account grew increasingly labyrinthine, weaving narratives of beings that defied material form—luminous entities that existed in an eternal state of becoming, designed to oversee the evolution of consciousness across time's vast, unseen currents. She spoke of Lawrence's final days—they were not days of retreat or exile, but of preparation. Lawrence had believed that the deserts, the empty spaces of ancient certainty, concealed keys not just to history, but to existence itself. He called it Sahra Al-Zaman, Edith revealed, her voice trembling with reverence. The Desert of Time. It's a metaphysical plane where all possibilities converge—past, present, future—held together like threads in a cosmic tapestry. Lawrence understood that certain landscapes are woven from the very fibers of the infinite, and that he was merely a custodian tasked with guarding the threshold. Each word sounded like a piece of a grander puzzle, weaving Ahmed into a rapidly expanding web of realities lurking just beneath the surface of his rational mind.

Throughout the night, Edith's stories painted visions so vivid they seemed to shimmer in the silver moonlight—her descriptions of Lawrence pacing before fires, reciting sections of the Quran in flawless Arabic, or negotiating fiercely with figures unseen yet acutely felt, created a tableau of a man caught between worlds. She whispered of debates that would echo into eternity—Nancy Astor's sharp words, Sassoon's scribbled notes, Augustus John's restless sketches—all illuminated by the flickering flame of an unspoken understanding. And then, her tone shifted subtly, a shift from story to prophecy, as she disclosed her own role as a guardian of one such nexus—a point where time's flow became malleable, where the influence of entities from beyond the limits of linear existence lingered like whispers in the dark. Her final revelation was startling: Lawrence's retreat at Clouds Hill was no mere act of withdrawal but a deliberate act of investigation—an attempt to decipher, contain, and eventually harness these mysterious forces that ripple through Dorset's quiet landscape.

Ahmed's skepticism flickered, fragile and tentative, as Edith unveiled Lawrence's journals. The pages—fragile, trembling—carried the unmistakable mark of authenticity: handwritten notes dense with scientific-like sketches and cryptic annotations. The words seemed to pulse with energy—observations of chronological displacements, experiments with consciousness, sketches of bizarre, unearthly crafts. The journals delve deeper into Lawrence's belief that certain locations on Earth are more than mere geography; they are gateways, gateways that link the physical with the metaphysical, the temporal with the eternal. Ahmed felt a tremor in his conviction—these documents reshaped his understanding, whispering that the man revered as a colonizer might have been a pioneer of something far more profound, a fealty to truths that only the enlightened could perceive. It struck him that every line hinted at a knowledge so advanced that it bordered on mysticism—a knowledge that could shatter his entire worldview if fully understood.

Then Edith's voice grew softer, carrying a meaning that made Ahmed's breath catch. As she laid the journal open on the table, she pointed to a faded inscription—To S.A.—and explained that it referenced Sahra Al-Zaman, not a person but a concept. This was Lawrence's key—his personal code for a state of consciousness, a realm within the desert where time folded and space dissolved. Lawrence had learned that certain places on Earth, particularly the desert, were not just deserts but living membranes of energy—thresholds where linear time became porous. For Lawrence, the desert was more than landscape; it was a living, breathing entity, a vast reservoir of potentiality, waiting to be unlocked by those who truly understood its silent language. This revelation reshaped Ahmed's perception—what he had considered archaeological relics and historical curiosities now shimmered with the glow of a deeper, cosmic truth. Edith's words, full of reverence, made it clear that Lawrence's true mission was to safeguard these portals, to guide others toward understanding the shifting currents of eternity embedded within the earth itself.

As dawn approached, a faint hum began—an almost imperceptible vibration that radiated from the very core of the cottage, growing stronger with every passing minute. Edith's eyes widened, her hand trembling as she pointed skyward. The heavens above, once a quiet shroud of stars, fractured like a mirror—a mosaic of shifting, shimmering light, revealing facets of something vast, complex, and utterly beyond comprehension. The air thrummed with a melody no mortal ears could fully hear, a symphony of possibility that stretched across dimensions. Then, as if summoned by that unearthly resonance, silhouettes emerged—tall, luminous beings who shimmered against the breaking sky, their forms unfixed, like liquid sculptures of pure consciousness. They did not speak—words were unnecessary—they entered Ahmed's mind through currents of thought and feeling, revealing profound truths: these entities were guardians, sentinels of the cosmic pathways, watching over the evolution of awareness across countless realms. Their appearance marked the convergence of the finite and the infinite, a crossing point at the edge of all known reality.

What Ahmed experienced dwarfed every rational explanation—an immersion into a realm where time was liquid and consciousness the only map. These beings explained that Earth's future paths were carved by choices made in moments of heightened awareness—choices that could lead to awakening or destruction. The realization crested within him like a wave—humans had the innate ability to navigate the currents of the universe, to transcend the linear bounds set by history and biology. The entities conveyed that the human mind, when fine-tuned, could exchange signals with higher civilizations—custodians of the evolution of consciousness. As Ahmed's senses stretched into this uncharted ocean, he perceived that Lawrence's true role had been much larger than a military officer—he was a link, a bridge between the material and the divine, a firestarter in humanity's awakening to its infinite potential. The night seemed endless, yet in that moment, Ahmed grasped an undeniable truth: the artifacts, the journals, the landscapes—they all existed to guide souls toward understanding that reality itself was born from the depths of awareness, flowing like a cosmic tide that would forever shape the future of existence.

When consciousness slowly retracted, Ahmed found himself back in the ruined shell of the cottage, the first rays of dawn slicing through the debris, illuminating the ancient stones and the relics strewn across the floor. Yet, everything had subtly shifted. In the shadows, faintly glimmering, he discovered a small, faceted crystal—smooth, yet alive with a flickering internal glow. Its surface pulsed with rhythms that matched the resonance sealing his awakening. Carefully, he tucked it into his pocket, feeling the weight of unseen knowledge pressing against his skin. His hands trembled—not from fear, but from the profound realization of the role he was destined to play: defender of the gateways, messenger of the unseen currents, heir to Lawrence's unfulfilled mission. The landscapes outside remained quiet and bloodless, but beneath that silence, he sensed the endless ripple—waves of potential crashing through the fabric of the universe, waiting for those brave enough to listen and step into the unknown.

***

Five

Lady Edith's Chronicles

Whispers from the Edge of Time

The dim glow of the oil lamp flickered softly within Edith's drawing room, casting elongated shadows over a multitude of artifacts that seemed suspended in time. A heavy air of anticipation lingered as Lawrence's journals, bound in worn leather, lay open on a side table, their pages adorned with meticulous script that appeared to shimmer in the dim light. Edith, seated with a regal poise, looked across to Ahmed, her eyes reflecting the reverence of someone who had witnessed epochs firsthand. She spoke quietly, her voice weighted with the gravity of her revelations, describing the countless evenings when Lawrence would summon Sassoon and others to this very space—discussions that veered far beyond military strategy into realms unseen, where myth and reality intertwined like threads in a cosmic loom.

The room was filled with whispers of their dialogues, filled with fierce debates about colonial awakening and spiritual destiny. Edith recounted how Sassoon, with his characteristic candor, often challenged Lawrence's esoteric convictions, dismissing them as fanciful dreams of a poet turned explorer. Yet, beneath Sassoon's skepticism lay a grudging fascination, an unspoken acknowledgment that these gatherings were more than mere literary salons—they were meetings of minds intent on unlocking mysteries buried in the sands of history and consciousness. As Edith detailed the gathering's ambiance—the crackling fire, the scented tea, the faint aroma of myrrh mixed with smoke from burning oud—Ahmed felt a shiver crawl along his spine. Among the assembled, the presence of Augustus John's restless sketches and the delicate gleam of Bedouin silver hinted at a deeper purpose: that these individuals, driven by different passions, all sought to pierce the veils separating worlds.

She paused, then leaned forward with a measured breath, her voice becoming almost a whisper. Lawrence, more than anyone, knew that the desert's silence hid secrets—secrets that transcended time itself. Her words turned more fervent as she described how, during long nights, Lawrence would pace before the fireplace, reciting passages from the Quran with a voice so steady it seemed to carve into the very fabric of reality. Sassoon, scribbling furiously, had once remarked that Lawrence seemed haunted by distant echoes from beyond the known universe—echoes that beckoned him towards peculiar phenomena, incidents that defied logic and rational explanation. Edith's gaze grew distant as she recalled the debates that stretched into the early hours—discussions about the future of the Arab world, yes, but also about the very nature of existence. She revealed that Lawrence's retreat to Clouds Hill was not solely for respite, but to pursue what he called "the probing of the temporal currents," phenomena that had gripped his imagination and perhaps even his soul. An extraordinary notion—that the landscape of Dorset was a nexus, a point where the fabric of history and mud alike thinned to reveal the tapestry beneath.

***

The evening air grew thick with a sense of otherworldly expectancy as Edith's stories wove through the dimly lit cabin, the flickering candlelight casting elongated shadows on walls lined with relics of distant worlds. Her voice, soft yet charged with unspoken knowing, recounted how Lawrence's retreat—hidden within the Dorset landscape—was far more than a refuge from the banalities of routine; it was a nexus, a site where the veils between dimensions bled and suggestions of time's fluidity bled into the fabric of reality itself. The landscape outside seemed to pulse with this secret energy, the heather and gorse whispering in language older than words, calling to those who could listen beyond the surface. Ahmed's rational mind wrestled with the vividness of her descriptions, but each detail—each glance at the open window framing the moonlit heath—seemed to brush against a line of understanding stretching just beyond his grasp.

Edith's face greased with the patina of age and grace, was an emblem of the audience of forgotten histories she claimed to have witnessed. She leaned closer, her voice a hushed murmur, revealing her own initiation into this eldritch truth: that Lawrence's true mission was obscured by myth, cloaked in allegory, and rooted in phenomena that defied the compass of empirical science. She described how, beneath the tranquil exterior of Clouds Hill, Lawrence had engaged with forces that many dared not acknowledge—forces that hinted at the malleable, even unstable, nature of time itself. Her words conjured images of nights spent in silent vigil, watching the horizon as strange vapors drifted over the heath, shimmering with eldritch light that flickered in and out of existence like passing memories. She told him, with a careful, deliberate tone, that Lawrence's motorcycles, the relics of his rugged independence, were also keys—conduits—allowing him to venture into realms where geography and chronology blurred, leaving footprints across the fabric of reality.

As if summoned by her revelations, the quiet hum of the cottage grew into a palpable resonance—vibrations neither heard nor seen, but deeply felt, rippling through the core of Ahmed's consciousness. Edith gently reached into a cabinet, retrieving an old leather-bound journal, its cover embossed with symbols that seemed to shift whenever he focused on them. She placed it in his trembling hands, asserting that this was no replica but the very handwriting of Lawrence himself—an offer, perhaps, of proof or a challenge. The pages revealed meticulous entries, darkened with age yet vibrant in detail: accounts of times when Lawrence had witnessed "events outside linear flow," episodes where moments froze and then unfurled anew, histories that insisted on their own existence outside the confines of the record. Ahmed's eyes darted across the script, reading theories about consciousness—its capacity to shape and fracture time's seemingly unbreakable chain—while sketches of craft, unlike any aircraft known, fluttered like glyphs from another universe. Every word echoed a secret yearning to pierce the conventional, a whisper from the abyss suggesting that the past, present, and future are interwoven threads in a tapestry much larger than anyone believed.

Then Edith's voice lowered, her gaze fixing him in a hypnotic stare. She explained the true meaning behind Lawrence's cryptic dedication "To S.A." — not a mere homage to a person, but an abbreviation for "Sahra Al-Zaman," or "The Desert of Time," an idea that Lawrence had hidden within his texts, secreted away like a gem. It was a landscape not of sand and mirage, but of existential dimensions where the currents of time themselves could be navigated. The desert, she claimed, was a metaphysical arena—an intersection point.at which Earth's hidden ley lines converged, radiating strain and promise in equal measure. Lawrence, she said, had discerned that certain locations on the planet operated as portals, gateways shimmering at the edge of perception, allowing consciousness to slip across the boundaries of chronological linearity. The vast emptiness of deserts, especially that of Arabia and Dorset, served as keys to understanding that reality was more elastic than the mind was willing to accept, that human perception was but a thin veneer over a deeper, fluid truth.

Night deepened and Edith's tone took on an almost hypnotic quality, drawing Ahmed into a space where rationality dissolved into wonder. She recounted how Lawrence's obsession was not merely the chaos of war but the pursuit of these nexus points—places where time itself buckled and revealed glimpses of its infinite face. She told of her own childhood witnessing strange lights flickering along the horizon, of days when clocks inexplicably skipped forward or backward, and how Lawrence believed such anomalies were signs—signs he was determined to understand and, ultimately, to control. It was then that she produced a small, leather-bound box containing Lawrence's personal journals—discarded in a moment of peril and assumed lost forever. Opening one, she let Ahmed glimpse the pages; the handwriting was unmistakable, with a precision that betrayed a mind obsessed with the fabric of reality. The entries detailed experiments, notes on "chronal shifts," and cryptic sketches of craft that shimmered with a strange, iridescent sheen. These visions, she insisted, were more than mere notes—they were maps, keys to stepping beyond the limitations of human perception into realms that lay just beyond the veil of what is deemed possible.

What struck Ahmed most was the revelation that Lawrence's mysterious final message, written deep within those pages, referenced "Sahra Al-Zaman" explicitly. It was not simply poetic mysticism but an encoded directive, a call to locate the desert of time—a realm that Lawrence believed existed not as far-flung mythology but as a fundamental layer of reality itself. Edith explained how Lawrence's studies uncovered that certain regions—across the globe—served as natural "temporal nodes," points where history's fabric was thinner, more susceptible to distortion. These nodes, she said, were focal points in the Earth's subtle energetic web—triggers for what Lawrence called "the great convergence," moments when human consciousness could access higher dimensions of understanding if one knew how to listen. Her words, woven into the night, seemed to ripple through Ahmed's mind, unraveling layers of academic certainty he'd held for years, replacing them with a fluid sense of being in a universe where time was a malleable substance—and his thought spun with the realization that Lawrence had not merely been a soldier, but a pioneer who dared to probe the very boundaries of the cosmos itself.

Edith's voice softened further as she drew him outside into the cool night, whispering that Lawrence's motorcycle, the sleek, polished Brough Superior, was more than just a vehicle—an artifact of power and tradition. It was, she claimed, a conduit, a vessel capable of piercing the veil even at the most guarded nexus points. Ahmed saw the gleaming brass fittings, the well-oiled engine that seemed to hum with a strange resonance, almost alive. As he looked up at the star-studded sky, stretching infinitely beyond the confines of Earth, a sudden, inexplicable shift occurred. The heavens seemed to fracture like ancient parchment, lines of cosmic light ripping across the firmament, revealing glimpses of realms that defied logic. In that moment, standing amidst the relics of a forgotten voyager and the whispers of unseen forces, Ahmed felt a sensation that transcended physicality, the trembling acknowledgment that he was on the cusp of discovering something—something that threatened to rupture the fabric of his entire understanding of reality.

***

The air outside grew thick with an unsettling silence, as if the countryside itself held a breath in anticipation. Shadows lengthened across the uneven terrain, their shapes shifting subtly as the dying light cast a flickering pallor over the heathland. Ahmed's car coughed once, then remained dead—an inert metal sentinel that seemed oddly anchored to the landscape. Frustration and an inexplicable unease gnawed at him; he sensed that this was no ordinary roadside breakdown, but a juncture—an opening in the fabric of linearity itself. With every passing moment, he felt the boundaries between what was real and what lay just beyond becoming disturbingly porous.

As he stepped out into the cool dusk, the familiar landscape around Bovington Heath appeared to warp subtly under his gaze, as if the very ground beneath his feet remembered things it shouldn't. Rhododendrons and birch trees seemed to lean closer, their gnarled branches whispering secrets carried on a breeze that felt heavier with unseen intent. A faint shimmer flickered at the edge of his vision, like a reflection on water rippling before vanishing into the ether. Clutching his coat tightly, Ahmed moved toward the cottage—an irregular structure that defied the tidy symmetry of nearby buildings, its stones and woodwork hinting at ages passed, as though it had grown organically from the earth rather than been constructed by human hands.

Suddenly, a low, resonant hum vibrated through the air, not loud but perceptible—more felt than heard—registering directly into his consciousness. It was a sound without sound, an oscillation of reality that hinted at something fundamentally different, a ripple disturbing the persistent flow of time. Without conscious thought, Ahmed's eyes flicked upward, and he saw it—a fractured sky, the very fabric of the universe tearing at points, revealing glimpses of other realms layered just beneath the surface of perception. The stars twinkled with a strange intensity, yet movements among them defied the coalescence of natural law. This was no ordinary phenomenon; it was as if the cosmos itself was bending, revealing its hidden code, and pulling him into its cryptic depths.

The cottage's ancient door creaked open slowly, revealing Edith Carrington with a calm that contrasted sharply with the upheaval looming around them. Her eyes bore the depth of centuries, yet they sparkled with a vitality that suggested she knew the universe's most guarded secret. Her presence was an anchor amid the chaos, her composure lending both reassurance and a sense of gravitas. As she beckoned him inside, Ahmed realized that the boundaries between history and eternity had begun to dissolve—this was no ordinary meeting. Every moment in her company felt like a step into a realm where the past, present, and future converged into a single, luminous point. And he knew, without understanding how, that whatever awaited inside would forever alter his understanding of time itself.

The interior of the bungalow shimmered with an inexplicable glow, as if the walls pulsed with silent energy. First editions of Lawrence's favorite books shared shelves with relics from distant deserts—Persian miniatures, Bedouin silver—each artifact whispering stories that belonged to all ages simultaneously. The air was thick with potent aromas, notes of aged tea and secrets long kept from the world. Edith moved effortlessly, her voice weaving through the space as she recounted moments from Lawrence's clandestine meetings with Sassoon, John, and others whose names had become myths. Her stories painted a scene of late-night debates, recitations in perfect Arabic by Lawrence, and unspoken threads connecting them through a shared pursuit of forbidden knowledge. Yet beneath her words, a deeper truth lurked—one that hinted at dreams beyond the limits of linear time.

Then, she revealed the journals—Lawrence's handwritten volumes that, until now, had been considered lost to history. Each page crackled with age, but their ink remained vivid, the script flowing with a confident precision. The entries spoke of more than military strategies—they detailed what he called "chronological displacements," anomalies that bent the very fabric of moments, warping memories and projecting glimpses of worlds not yet born. Lawrence theorized that certain locations, like the vast deserts or isolated hills, acted as gateways—points where time could be traversed or even manipulated. His sketches of strange craft, drawn with a meticulousness that rivaled scientific diagrams, suggested technology not of this earth—a craft that defied conventional understanding, shimmering between light and matter as if it belonged to a different dimension altogether. Dreams and visions fused within the pages, forming a mosaic of a man who saw beyond the horizon of ordinary perception.

What gripped Ahmed most was the explanation behind the mysterious dedication "To S.A." in Seven Pillars of Wisdom. Edith's voice softened as she clarified that the initials referred not to a person, but to "Sahra Al-Zaman"—a concept as ancient as the dunes themselves, translating roughly to "The Desert of Time." This was a realm Lawrence believed to exist at the edges of human consciousness, a space where the sands of eternity shifted and merged with the fabric of reality. Lawrence, she claimed, had discovered this metaphysical landscape through his encounters in the Arabian deserts—places where the horizon's mirage cloaked access to unseen currents flowing beneath the surface of existence. These currents, Lawrence surmised, connected all points in space and time, forming a vast web that could be navigated by those attuned to its subtle signals. The desert, with its endless emptiness and shifting sands, was nothing less than a gateway—an aperture into the "Sahra," a space where past and future folded into the present like a scroll unrolling in the wind.

By now, the atmosphere in the bungalow had transformed into something intangible, palpable only through intuition. Edith's stories grew darker, infused with a sense of warning. She spoke of being a guardian—one bound to protect the portals that linked the world's hidden currents. She revealed her own role as a custodian of this delicate balance, and how she had watched Lawrence's experiments creep beyond the scope of mere exploration, into the realm of manipulation. His investigations, she warned, had attracted attention beyond the human domain—beings and entities not bound by linear time, watching and waiting. Their gaze lingered on Earth's shifting thresholds, and Lawrence had sought to understand their influence, perhaps even to commune with them. Now, as the night deepened beyond belief, Edith's words became spectral, drifting into a space where words stopped and what remained was pure resonance.

At precisely 3:17 AM—what Edith called "Lawrence's hour"—a subtle, harmonic vibration unfurled across the landscape, stirring something in Ahmed's core. Stepping outside, he was met with a scene impossible to describe: the sky itself fractured into ribbons of shimmering uncertainty, revealing glimpses of worlds spun from pure light. Above the cottage, shapes emerged—tall, luminous beings that seemed to shimmer beyond physical form. Their presence transcended normal perception, manifesting as waves of consciousness that brushed against Ahmed's mind, infusing him with visions of higher existence. They communicated in a symphony of thoughts and images, sharing truths too vast and subtle for language, truths that suggested they were custodians of evolution—not merely of species, but of awareness itself.

These entities explained that Earth's current state teetered on the edge of a critical evolutionary phase, a point where human consciousness would either ascend into a cosmic unity or fall apart under its own ignorance. Their role, they said, was to monitor and guide these processes—standing guard at the thresholds of time, guarding Pietà portals that could bring enlightenment or chaos. Their message was clear: the earth's fabric was woven with multiple probability pathways, each a ripple in an infinite pond of potentialities. Types of futures flickered before Ahmed—worlds where humanity thrived as an awakened collective, shining in awareness, and others where it plunged into darkness, distracted and divided. The beings reached into his mind, projecting images of heroes and villains, of civilizations born from consciousness and civilizations destroyed by neglect. For the first time, Ahmed glimpsed the universe not as a fixed stage but as a liquid ocean of possibility, where everything depended on the quality of awareness present at each moment.

He sensed that consciousness was no longer a mere attribute but the very essence of creation—an energetic force that, if understood, could shape worlds. In that cosmic exchange, he felt the thin threads of his own identity stretch and dissolve, blending into the vast tapestry of interconnected awareness. When he finally regained his senses, the luminous beings had vanished, leaving behind only the echo of their parting message: the future was fluid, and the human mind held the key. As dawn approached, Ahmed found himself back inside the ruined cottage, clutching a small, pulsating crystal reminiscent of the visions—an artifact left behind by the guardians, a fragment of the fabric they had woven into his consciousness. The landscape was silent once more, the fractured sky weaving in and out, but within him bloomed a new understanding: that the true power lay in awareness, and that beyond the shadows of linear time, a vast, unfolding mystery awaited those willing to perceive its depths.

***

Six

Unveiling the Journals

Words that Bridge Dimensions

The earliest pages of Lawrence's journals exuded an unassuming sobriety at first glance—spidery ink coursing across yellowed parchment, each stroke precise yet imbued with an almost restless energy. As Ahmed's eyes traveled across the lines, the rigid mechanical cadence of the words softened into a rhythm that felt both archaic and profoundly alive. It was as if the handwriting itself carried a pulse, revealing a mind unshackled from linear constraints, emboldened in its pursuit of truths beyond the mere chronological. The ink bore the faint scent of ancient earth, of secret oils and sun-baked desert wind, whispering silent keys to a universe far beyond the confines of conventional history. The script's irregularities—occasional slips, the slight tremble of certain loops—spoke of a hand often moving in tandem with unseen currents, as if Lawrence's consciousness were translating itself through the very act of inscription, bridging worlds unseen by ordinary senses.

Within that delicate scrawl lay revelations that challenged every certainty Ahmed had carried into this strange refuge. The pages brimmed with detailed accounts of phenomena that defied the laws of physics—references to "chronological displacements," "temporal vortices," and "moments flung out of sequence," inscribed in a language that fused scientific inquiry with poetic insight. Lawrence's words read less like military reports and more like the manuscripts of a mad scientist or a mystic, weaving laboratory measurements with whispers of divine intention. It was as if each sentence hinted at a hidden map, an intricate pattern of universe-layered realities that only those willing to see beyond the surface could begin to fathom. The handwriting's authenticity was undeniable—every curve, every angle confirmed that these were the writings of a man who had glimpsed something vastly larger than himself, a truth that lurked just beyond the edge of perception.

The discovery of these journals was no accidental find. Edith, with her aristocratic poise and knowing smile, had handed them over as if passing a sacred relic—an artifact that bridged the gaps between myth, memory, and the present moment. As Ahmed traced the flow of Lawrence's ink, her voice echoed softly, describing Lawrence's obsession not merely with conquest but with the fabric of time itself—how certain locations in the Arabian deserts and the Dorset landscape had acted as anchors or gateways, where reality's seams thinned. She explained that Lawrence's journey into the unknown was driven by a consciousness that recognized the universe's underlying malleability, its fabric woven with currents that could be navigated by those whose minds had awakened to their true nature. She spoke of a man who, despite his outward persona, had been a seeker threading through dimensions, chasing the elusive threads that tethered worlds and times together—an explorer of the invisible currents beneath the surface of history.

The real shock came when Edith reached into a concealed drawer, unveiling a folded manuscript, the edges ragged and stained yet undeniably authentic. It was Lawrence's own handwriting, a sprawling script that seemed to ripple with fervor, detailing experiments with "temporal stabilization" and "cosmic consciousness"—terms that sounded almost absurd in the traditional military context. But within these pages lay theories that could reframe the entire understanding of history. Lawrence's notes described craft whose sketches resembled biological organisms more than machines, their forms shifting between matter and energy—objects that moved through a labyrinth of reality, not along linear paths but through intricate pathways only perceptible to those aware of the universe's true architecture. Here, amid the ink, was a map of the unseen—a blueprint for navigation through a multidimensional cosmos. Ahmed's rational mind recoiled in disbelief; he questioned whether his scholarly training was sufficient to grasp these depths. Yet, deep inside, a whisper of recognition stirred—an echo of truths he had always sensed but dared not articulate.

***

In the hushed silence of the bungalow's dim interior, Lady Edith unfolded a fragile, leather-bound volume that seemed untouched by time, as though it had been waiting here for its awakening. Her delicate fingers traced the inked curves of the handwritten pages, each stroke trembling with the weight of history and hidden truths. Ahmed stared, feeling a strange dissonance—this was no ordinary manuscript; it bore the unmistakable candor of Lawrence's own hand, its ink imbued with a life beyond mere words. The pages seemed to pulse subtly, as if alive, whispering secrets in a language older than the centuries they spanned, beckoning him into depths he scarcely dared to navigate.

Within those lines, Franco's meticulous script detailed observations that surpassed the scope of traditional military intelligence—notes that read more like scientific reports, filled with references to phenomena that defied what he had believed about time and space. Lawrence's handwriting spoke of "displacement events," moments when reality shimmered, unmooring itself from the sequence of linear days. As Ahmed's eyes darted across the pages, he sensed that what was written challenged the entire foundation of his scholarly understanding—here was a narrative not just of campaigns and politics but of consciousness itself, spilling into realms where history folded into mystery.

The quiet rustling of paper was suddenly punctuated by Edith's steady voice, as she explained that these writings were not mere remnants of a lost life but keys—clues pointing toward a hidden architecture of reality. She revealed that Lawrence believed certain locations harbored the potential to slip through the cracks of linear time, revealing glimpses of eternity for those who dared to look. The journals, she claimed, documented a nascent science of the soul—a blueprint for those who could accept that beyond the veneer of history lay an intricate web of unseen currents. With each word, a fragment of Ahmed's rational veneer cracked, splintering into shadows where doubt and wonder intertwined into an intoxicating doubt.

As Edith carefully lifted a yellowed sheet from the stack, a sudden stillness suffused the room—an almost sacred anticipation, as though the air itself held its breath. The sketch was crude yet disturbing in its precision: an outline of a craft unlike anything known, draped in flowing geometries that seemed to vibrate between solidity and liquid light. Ahmed's breath hitched as he scrutinized the drawing; the contours shimmered, shifting subtly beneath his gaze, revealing forms that seemed to transcend physical laws—objects that hovered on the brink of perception, carrying within them an echo of other dimensions. These sketches weren't merely artifacts; they felt like invitations, summons from a higher order.

From the edges of the paper, faint halos of luminescence flickered, as if the imagery itself pulsed with consciousness. Edith's voice broke his trance, speaking of Lawrence's obsession with "unseen crafts," pointing to their possible origin beyond Earth, beyond the known universe. The diagrams depicted structures that bent space and time, machines that seemed to modulate the very fabric of existence. The lines of the drawings held a rhythm—an ancient melody encoded visually, hinting at technological marvels woven into the tapestry of metaphysics. Ahmed could feel the weight of this revelation pressing down, a breathless certainty that the boundary between science and mysticism was thinner than he'd ever suspected.

Later that night, beneath a sky dusted with invisible currents of starlight, Edith's voice dipped into whispers of her own encounters—visions of Lawrence, journeying not only through deserts of shifting sand but across horizons where time unfurled in infinite ribbons. Her words painted a landscape of metaphysical significance, a "Desert of Time" that wasn't merely a geographical place but a threshold—a space where the trajectories of history, consciousness, and destiny intertwined like threads in an eternal loom. She explained that Lawrence's obsession with that empty expanse was rooted in this deeper awareness: the desert's empty vastness concealed a portal into what he called "Sahra Al-Zaman," a realm where moments could dance, overlap, and dissolve into one another.

Ahmed stood on the edge of this revelation, feeling the pull of the mystical as it brushed against his rational mind. Edith's stories described how Lawrence had traveled to these nexus points, not with conventional weapons or strategies but with the intent to glimpse the fabric of eternity itself—drawing power from the silent, ancient energies embedded within the sands. Those energies, she claimed, were manifestations of a cosmic web—an unfathomable net of interwoven time streams that could be harnessed or simply observed, if one possessed the courage to see beyond the illusion of linearity. This was not merely history; it was a revelation of the universe as a living, breathing occurrence, where every thought, every decision, resonated through boundless layers of existence.

Over the hours that followed, Edith's narrative intensified into an incantation of urgency and sacred duty. She handed Ahmed a yellowed, fragile sheet—the last note Lawrence ever left behind, penned in the flowing Arabic script that seemed to glow softly when touched by subtle light. The words, faint yet resonant, read simply: "Find Sahra Al-Zaman." For the first time, Ahmed understood that these words weren't an ambiguous poetic metaphor but a directive—a summons to locate the metaphysical desert that sat at the intersection of worlds. It was the key to understanding Lawrence's true voyage, a journey that transcended armies and alliances to touch the core of existence itself.

The dawn's first light seeped through the cracked windowpanes, casting long shadows that seemed to dance with the flickering remnants of the night's visions. As Ahmed touched the paper, a strange vibration coursed through his fingertips—a whisper of resonance that hinted at truths lying just beyond reach. Edith's final words lingered in his mind like a melody—"the desert is a state of consciousness"—and suddenly he felt the fragile barrier of his skepticism trembling, threatening to crumble altogether. All that he knew, all he had claimed to understand, now seemed fragile and incomplete.

In that moment, a flicker of movement outside caught his eye—a shimmer across the garden, as if the very air itself was rippling in response to the unspoken call. His heart quickened as he peered into the shadows, senses sharpening. The garden, silent and still, concealed a secret deeper than the roots of the ancient trees—an opening into the unseen, a portal whispering promises of infinity, waiting to be crossed. In the silence that followed, Ahmed realized that his journey into the shadows had only just begun, and that the true adventure lay beyond whatever illusions of time and history he had long accepted. The only question now was whether he possessed the courage to step through the opening, into the boundless, whispering darkness of Sahra Al-Zaman.

***

As midnight draped its heavy velvet over Bovington Heath, the silence seemed to pulse with unseen rhythms, an almost imperceptible throb that resonated in the marrow of the land itself. Dr. Ahmed Ridha stepped carefully through the debris-strewn garden, eyes fixed upon the faint shimmer that had appeared just moments before, a dance of light spilling from the jagged fissures in the universe's fabric. The air was thick with the scent of impending change, a mixture of damp earth and something undefinable—an echo of other times, of memories layered upon memories which refused to surrender to the linear flow of history. Every leaf, every stone seemed imbued with a whisper of secrets, as if the very landscape conceived of itself as a living mosaic of unseen currents, rippling beneath the surface of the known world.

Underneath the fractured sky, Ahmed's gaze was drawn upward, where the heavens warped in a pattern that defied classical geometry—an unfolding tapestry of fractal motifs shimmering with hues beyond the visible spectrum. A crystalline construct materialized amidst the constellations, its surface morphing between solidity and liquid light, as if striving to embody the paradoxes of existence itself. The ripples of this anomaly spread outward, twisting the very fabric of space in a dance of chaos and order—a mutating canvas where forms obeyed no law but their own. At the heart of this celestial spectacle, vague silhouettes emerged, enigmatic giants whose luminous forms shimmered with intelligence unfathomable, a consciousness that seethed beyond words or understanding. These beings, entities of pure awareness, communicated through waves of thought that reverberated in Ahmed's mind, a language of the soul spun from storms of intention and memory.

Soaked in awe and dread, Ahmed realized that this was no fleeting illusion but an invitation—an opening into a domain where time dissolved and possibility expanded into infinity. The beings explained without words, their presence a rippling thought—an invitation to see beyond history's slender confines into a realm of boundless potential. They showed him visions of terrestrial points where temporal currents converged—a crossroads where worlds bled into one another, creating corridors of eternity that flowed like unseen rivers beneath the Earth's surface. It became clear that Lawrence's mysterious obsession with the desert had been no mere quest for adventure but a conscious navigation of these intersections, where reality's crust grew thin and the essence of time itself shimmered like a mirage. The understanding sank deep into Ahmed's bones: this was the core of his true inheritance—an inheritance built upon the unspoken sketches of unfamiliar craft, etched not on paper but in the very fabric of the universe, revealing visions of other realms just beyond perception's reach.

He watched as the luminous beings moved among the fractured stars, their forms flickering in and out of visibility—phantoms of thought sculpted in starlight and shadow. Their whispers filled the void, untranslatable yet deeply felt, guiding him through corridors not of space but of consciousness. In this moment, time itself unfurled into a liquid tapestry—currents flowing from past to future, from possibility to reality—each ripple a choice, a chance event, a fragment of eternity. Ahmed's mind expanded, memories of scholarly detachment dissolving into a flood of genuine understanding. Here, in the quiet chaos of the cosmos, he glimpsed the true architecture of existence: a symphony composed not in sound but in thought, a geometric language that spoke directly to the spirit. The beings beckoned him forward, as if inviting him into their own perpetual becoming, urging him to recognize that Earth's most sacred secrets—those woven into the endless tapestry—were accessible only to those willing to navigate the invisible currents of the unseen realms.

As the cosmic dance reached its crescendo, the sky distorted into an aperture, revealing a beyond that shimmered with impossible geometries—dimensions layered one upon another, revealing the intricate mosaic of multiversal pathways. From within the depths of this kaleidoscope emerged a craft of staggering beauty, a vessel that seemed to imitate both matter and light in a impossibly fluid harmony. Its surface pulsed with a rhythm that echoed the heartbeat of the universe itself, shifting between physicality and vapor, between presence and absence. Ahmed's senses were flooded with a symphony of sensations—colors he had no names for, sounds that vibrated in the marrow of his bones—serving as the prelude to a journey that would fracture his understanding of reality itself. Somewhere within the silent depths, the luminous entities conveyed that this craft was both a tool and a key—an overlap point where the terrestrial and celestial, the temporal and the eternal, could intersect at will. It was no accident that these beings, guardians beyond form, had chosen him to witness this tableau—a portal into the uncharted territories of consciousness and existence, where sketches of unfamiliar craft offered glimpses into the vast beyond, whispering truths that dared not be spoken aloud but stained the soul with their indelible presence.

***

Seven

The "Desert of Time"

Myth, Reality, and the Unseen Frontier

The words on the tattered page, "To S.A."—a concise, almost cryptic inscription—hang like a whisper suspended in the quiet of the dimly lit study. At first glance, it seems a simple homage, a fleeting signature etched by a man whose life was entwined with the fabric of world history. Yet beneath that surface lies a riddle, an invitation to peer beyond the mere sequence of letters into a realm where language becomes a key rather than a cage. Ahmed's fingers trace the worn ink, feeling the weight of silence that accompanies it—an echo of intentions buried in layers of meaning that defy the superficial grasp of scholarly scrutiny. The phrase, he realizes, is not just a dedication but a portal to something altogether larger, more expansive, calling for interpretation that transcends literal translation.

As the storm of his doubts settles, Ahmed's mind begins to tease apart the layers of symbolism embedded in those two letters. "S.A."—a seemingly straightforward abbreviation—resonates deeper when viewed through the lens of the metaphysical. Could it, he ponders, be a cipher? Not merely the initials of a person, but perhaps an acronym stretching into the secret vocabulary of the desert—an encoded fragment of a hidden language, a signpost pointing toward a realm where time and space blur into one continuous current. Lawrence, with his reputation for obscurity and his flirtation with the esoteric, may have intentionally crafted this dedication as a kind of coded compass, guiding future seekers to the "desert of time," Sahra Al-Zaman—an unseen frontier that exists not on any map, but within the consciousness of those daring enough to search for it.

In the dim glow, Edith's voice, rich with quiet authority, begins to weave vivid imagery, transforming the scholarly puzzle into a luminous vision. She describes Lawrence's obsession not solely with the Arab world but with the uncharted territories at the edge of human perception—spaces where memories and futures coalesce, where the very fabric of reality is malleable. The desert, she explains, had revealed to Lawrence its secret: a place where time itself is fluid, a vast undulating sea that can be navigated not through machines or conventional protocols, but through awareness and intent. The phrase "To S.A.", therefore, becomes an evocation—a poetic summons—calling anyone who encounters it to look beyond the surface and step into that fluid domain, where consciousness is the vessel and the desert the infinite horizon of potentialities.

Ahmed's heart quickens as Edith's stories paint a landscape not only of history but of invisible currents threading through space and mind. He envisions Lawrence pacing the flickering hearth of Clouds Hill, reciting passages from the Quran in a language that feels as ancient as the stars, connected to the silent whispers of the desert winds. The notion gnaws at him that Lawrence's true mission extended far beyond military exploits—a clandestine pilgrimage into realms where linear time fractures into fractals of possibility. The simple phrase, "To S.A.", now awakens as a sacred cipher, summoning explorers of the unseen—to interpret more than words, to grasp the shape of a vast, unseen universe that pulses beneath the veneer of history. Within this revelation lies a challenge: to see the dedication not as a mere inscription, but as an open door to understanding that time, like the desert, is a living, breathing entity—one that can be traversed when the mind learns to recognize its infinite pathways.

As the night intensifies and shadows deepen, Edith's voice takes on a tone of solemn reverence. She recounts how Lawrence's investigation into the "desert of time" led him into encounters with beings who exist beyond the constraints of space and moment—guardians of the transition points where linearity dissolves into consciousness. These entities, luminous and silent, communicate through impressions felt rather than heard, transmitting truths that challenge the very foundation of rational thought. Lawrence, Edith claims, was not merely a soldier of the earth but an unintentional seeker of the multidimensional—his dedication a beacon for those who understand that the true poetry of the desert lies in its power to shift perception. The phrase becomes less a label and more an invocation, urging future explorers to recognize the metaphysical terrain lurking beneath the superficial layers of reality, where the "desert of time" whispers secrets to those patient enough to listen, and brave enough to see beyond the illusions of linear history.

In the hush that follows, Edith gently produces a battered leather-bound journal, fragile yet imbued with the palpable weight of history. Its pages, penned in Lawrence's unmistakable hand, reveal an understanding that defies the constraints of normal view—scientific reports woven with symbols and diagrams suggesting experiments that defy conventional physics. Some sketches depict craft unlike anything seen in the early 20th century—shapes that morph between machines and living substance, hinting at higher-dimensional phenomena.

"These illustrations, she says softly, are not mere doodles but maps—visual keys to the unseen currents Lawrence wished future minds to decode. The pages speak of "temporal displacements," "cyclical patterns," and "dimensions where past and future intertwine"—all embedded within a language that resists reduction to mere words. The dedication, therefore, can be read as a literal call to action, a metaphysical summons encoded in the very fabric of written history, beckoning the reader toward the understanding that the desert's true secret is that time itself can be re-imagined—reconceived as a malleable force accessible through perception and consciousness."

Night deepens, and with it comes a sense of profound awakening—a sudden shift that feels as if reality itself begins to ripple. Edith's voice becomes softer, yet more charged with meaning. She speaks of her own role as a guardian, a custodian of these hidden gateways that Lawrence once sought and partially unlocked. The landscape around the cottage seems to pulse with unseen life, the air thickening with the resonance of long-forgotten truths. The phrase "To S.A." now echoes within Ahmed's mind, no longer as a perplexing abbreviation but as a vibrant, living symbol—an invitation to venture inward, to decode the whisperings of the desert within his own consciousness. The challenge is clear: interpret the dedication not through the lens of logic alone but through the intuitive recognition that beneath every symbol lies an entire universe waiting to be accessed. This realization is both a revelation and a burden—a calling that demands he look beyond the surface, into the depths where the unseen currents of time and awareness flow silently, forever beckoning explorers into realms that only the brave can navigate.

***

The landscape surrounding Bovington Heath stretched out in a muted tapestry of browns and greens, an endless horizon where the sky bowed low, heavy with the weight of impending rain. Dusk cast elongated shadows across the undulating heath, each blade of grass and gnarled branch whispering secrets of ages past—remnants of ancient energies lingering beneath the soil. As Ahmed's vehicle sputtered and finally faltered, a strange foreboding settled over him, as if the very earth had conspired to lead him to an unseen threshold. The sound of distant thunder mingled with the rhythmic pounding of his own heart, echoing like a muffled drumbeat in the vast silence. Standing outside, he felt the prickling sensation of being watched, the air thickening with the unspoken weight of histories yet to be unveiled.

His gaze drifted across the landscape, searching for any sign—an anomaly amid the mundane—when his eyes settled on a peculiar structure. Hidden among clusters of silver birches and moss-laden rhododendrons, a ramshackle bungalow emerged, its Arts and Crafts architecture a stark departure from the nearby military relics and the rough-hewn earth. Its weathered shingles whispered of decades, perhaps centuries, of secret lives interrupted by storms and shifting sands. Warm golden light spilled through stained glass panels, painting flickering patches onto the damp ground. A figure sat on the veranda—an elderly woman with a posture that suggested aristocratic fibres woven into her very bones—her gaze fixed upon the encroaching dark, patient as a guardian awaiting an unanticipated visitor.

With hesitant steps, Ahmed approached, each footfall crunching softly on the gravel. As he neared, the woman turned her head and offered a smile edged with familiar composure—grace, authority, a trace of inscrutable history. She introduced herself as Lady Edith Carrington, her voice mellow yet imbued with the unhurried rhythm of a life spent among the echoes of the past. She welcomed him inside, her manner effortless but layered with unspoken significance. Inside, the bungalow defied superficial modesty; shelves lined with first editions—Burton, Doughty, and Persian miniatures—clung to walls that seemed to hum with stories of an uncharted inner world. Artifacts from distant lands, Bedouin silver and ancient maps, hinted at journeys beyond the veil of time, as if each object was a fragment of a larger, cosmic puzzle awaiting the patient touch of a true seeker.

As the storm outside intensified, Edith poured a cup of rare pu-erh, its earthy aroma filling the air with an elusive promise. Her stories unraveled amid sips of the potent tea, like threads weaving through the fabric of his rational mind, challenging his academic certainties. She spoke of Lawrence not merely as a figure in history but as a man whose retreat at Clouds Hill concealed a fervent investigation into the very fabric of reality. She recounted how Lawrence would wander in the moonlit nights, reciting Arabic poetry by the fireplace while Sassoon sketched in his notebook and Augustus John observed with restless eyes. The tales hinted at a world beyond the known—an invisible tapestry connecting moments, voices, and dreams across the span of centuries. Edith's tone grew more evocative as she described Lawrence's obsession with "Sahra Al-Zaman," the Desert of Time, a metaphysical space that opened only to those who dared pierce the surface of history and step into its unseen currents.

Then, almost as if the shadows themselves had summoned her to reveal a deeper secret, Edith opened a battered leather-bound volume—Lawrence's journals, long believed lost in the chaos of the Suez Canal incident. The pages, filled with meticulous handwriting, shimmered with a resonance that seemed to hum with their own life. Descriptions of "chronological displacement events"—moments where time itself seemed to warp or leap—began to unfurl. Lawrence's observations read less like military reports and more like scientific experiments of consciousness, recounting visions of craft moving through dimensions, and theories proposing that some earthly locations are fertile grounds for temporal manipulation. Sketches appeared, rendered in charcoal and ink, depicting devices that defied technological norms—composites of metal, liquid light, and impossible geometries—standing as silent witnesses to experiments that transcended the boundaries of science and magic.

What truly unsettled Ahmed was Edith's interpretation of the famous dedication "To S.A." in Lawrence's "Seven Pillars of Wisdom." The phrase had long been dismissed as a humble tribute—yet Edith claimed it to be an encrypted reference to the "Sahra Al-Zaman." A space, a realm within the desert's heart, where the Earth's surface folds into the flowing fabric of time itself. She explained how Lawrence believed certain geographical points on the planet serve as intersections of these temporal currents, gateways to realms where past, present, and future coalesce in a chaos of infinite possibility. The desert, in this light, was not merely a barren expanse but a living, breathing node in a cosmic network—an unseen frontier that Lawrence dared to glimpse, and which now beckoned Ahmed to understand its true nature.

As darkness deepened, Edith's narrative took on an almost ritualistic quality. She described her lifelong role as a custodian of these nexus points, as one of the guardians tasked with observing the delicate dance of time's hidden flows. Her words suggested that Lawrence's true mission extended far beyond military conquest or colonial ambition; it was a profound dialogue with these intentional anomalies—probes into the structure of reality itself. She hinted at beings, entities of pure consciousness, and civilizations that had evolved beyond matter, all monitoring humanity's spiritual evolution through these ceaseless corridors. Her stories painted a universe filled with currents of energy, where certain individuals—mystics, scholars, warriors—had the rare capacity to traverse these unseen pathways, becoming conduits between worlds.

Finally, Edith looked skyward, her eyes reflecting the darkening heavens filled with shifting stars and fractured constellations. At precisely 3:17 AM—what she called "Lawrence's hour"—a harmonic resonance stirred the silence; an invitation from the beyond to cross into the threshold. Ahmed, instinctively drawn, stepped outside onto the damp veranda, feeling the air thicken and pulse with an intangible rhythm. Above Clouds Hill, the fabric of space seemed to shudder, revealing a fracture in the cosmos—an opening of shimmering, indescribable light. From this aperture emerged a craft, no ordinary vessel, but a shifting entity composed of liquid crystal and luminous metals, existing simultaneously in multiple states of matter. Its surface rippled like a liquid mirror, reflecting worlds beyond perception, while the air around it thrummed with reverberations—echos of other dimensions layered atop our own.

Then, without warning, entities descended—tall, luminous beings with forms that shimmered beyond human understanding. Their presence filled Ahmed with a longing he couldn't quite grasp, an awakening that bypassed words and entered directly into the core of his consciousness. They communicated through waves of thought, offering images: vast civilizations beyond our linear time, cosmic evolution, and the fragile web of consciousness connecting everything. These guardians explained their purpose: to oversee Earth's evolution, to steward the bridge between physical and metaphysical realms, and to prepare the planet—and individuals like Lawrence and himself—for a moment of critical convergence. As Ahmed's perception expanded, he realized he was no longer merely an observer but an active participant in this unfolding cosmic ballet. Every thought, every breath, became a ripple in the infinite ocean of possibility, and he understood—this was the place where destiny and eternity entwined, right at the crossroads of the universe's secret dimensions.

***

The landscape stretched before him, an endless tableau of shifting sands and fractured light, where the boundary between the tangible and the unseen blurred into a shimmering mirage. As Ahmed's gaze traced the horizon, a sudden chill coursed through him, as if some ancient force stirred beneath the earth's surface, whispering secrets only the soul could hear. The desert—silent and vast—carried within it a duality as old as time itself: the merciful, offering refuge to the wandering, and the malign, testing the very limits of human endurance. Here, the power of the desert was not merely in its scorching breath, but in its capacity to conceal and reveal, to be both sanctuary and trial, depending on the eye that perceives it.

Within the mind's eye, Ahmed saw the shifting sands as a canvas painted by forces beyond comprehension—currents of energy that course through unseen veins, shaping destinies as easily as wind sculpts dunes. The desert's silent vastness seemed to breathe—its breath a paradox, swelling with life and death alike. The heat of the day had long since ebbed; now, under a moonlight that cast shadows darker than ink, the desert revealed its other nature. Here, shadows stretched like serpents across the sands, promising both danger and salvation, embodying the very essence of duality that governed its spirit. It was a place haunted by the ghosts of history, yet alive with the promise of transformation, whispering that every grain of sand held within it a fragment of eternity.

Lady Edith's words echoed softly in Ahmed's mind, her voice tinted with the authority of one who knew the desert's secrets firsthand.

"This land, Mr. Ridha," she had said, her eyes shimmering with unspoken truths, "is both a malefic force and a well of mercy. It devours the unwary, stripping away illusion and ego, exposing the raw core of consciousness. Yet, for those brave enough to listen, it bestows gifts—visions of what lies beyond the veil of time."

Her description resonated with a strange resonance, stirring within Ahmed a deep sense of both dread and longing. The desert's power, she explained, was a mirror—reflecting aspects of the self long buried beneath layers of historical myth and subconscious distortion. Its duality was not a contradiction but a necessary harmony, balancing destruction and creation in a dance as old as existence itself.

The night's deeper darkness seemed to thicken in response, the silence so complete that one could hear the faint whispers of distant memories—epochs long forgotten, civilizations that had risen and fallen, all echoing through the eternal sands. In that silent void, Ahmed felt a presence—neither benevolent nor malevolent in the traditional sense, but something far more complex. It was as if the desert itself was alive, a sentient force allowing glimpses into the infinite possibilities of existence. The same sands that could swallow a soul into oblivion also held the power to elevate it, provided one understood the language of its dual nature. That language, Edith hinted, was one of introspection, humility, and willingness to confront one's own shadows—an act that could unravel the very fabric of linear time and reveal a hidden realm beneath.

As the dawn's first light tinged the horizon with a faint, bruised gold, Ahmed found himself questioning the very notion of power. Was the desert's malign aspect a form of vigilant cruelty, designed to weed out the weak from the worthy? Or was it, perhaps, a merciful gateway—an unyielding teacher guiding the conscious seeker toward an awakening far beyond the limits of ordinary perception? Edith's stories, rich with the voices of those who had traversed its depths, painted a picture not of static forces but of a dynamic interplay—an ongoing dialogue between light and shadow, chaos and order. It struck him that the desert's true nature might not be an external entity at all, but an inward mirror reflecting the nature of the human spirit. To gaze into it was to face oneself, with all the hidden darkness and divine radiance that entails.

The landscape, though stark and seemingly indifferent, pulsed with an underlying vitality—a secret fundament signaling that all dualities are woven from the same fabric. The malefic winds that tore through the dunes carried forewarnings, yet within their ferocity lay the seed of renewal. The dry, sunburned earth demanded a price; it demanded surrender, and in that surrender, offered the chance for transcendence. The environment itself, in its relentless dichotomy, held the blueprint for understanding the balance between destruction and salvation—each a necessary component of the other in maintaining the sacred harmony of existence. Ahmed sensed that beneath this rugged veneer lay a template of cosmic wisdom, waiting to be deciphered for those willing to surrender their illusions and embrace the paradoxes at the heart of reality.

He recalled Edith's quiet assertion that the desert was a living oracle—an unspoken oracle that tested with every step, revealing the true measure of a seeker's intention. Those who entered naïvely were swallowed, their egos shattered by the merciless trials. But those who approached with humility, curiosity, and reverence might unlock the hidden gateways—the thin places where time thins and the flow of consciousness becomes unbounded. The power of the desert was not merely in its physical might, but in its capacity to serve as a crucible—a forge where the soul's raw material was melted, refined, and shaped into something greater. That duality of threat and mercy, danger and salvation, formed the core of its eternal lesson: evolution requires confrontation with the shadow, yet it leads toward the luminous truth concealed within.

Awaiting the night's end, Ahmed stood at the precipice of understanding, his senses heightened by Edith's stories and his own subconscious stirrings. His gaze lingered on the horizon, where the rising sun would soon fracture the sky, casting light on secrets long hidden beneath the sands of time. The desert's power, he realized, was an invitation—a test that beckoned only the truly courageous. To walk its surface was to walk the edge of chaos and order simultaneously, dancing on the knife's edge between worlds seen and unseen. In that delicate balance lay the potential for rebirth—the rebirth of consciousness that Lawrence once glimpsed in the vast, empty expanse. The question now gnawed at him: was he destined to be merely a witness, or would he, too, become a keeper of the desert's dual truths—its merciful nurturing and its malign challenge—forever intertwined in the eternal dance of the cosmos?

***

Eight

Guardians of the Nexus

The Keepers of Unseen Currents

In the dim glow of dawn, the land around Bovington Heath seemed to pulse with an unseen rhythm—an inaudible hum that vibrated beneath the surface of the waking world. Ahmed, standing amidst the remnants of yesterday's revelations, felt the weight of a truth both ancient and unsettling pressing into his consciousness. The landscape, with its whispering grasses and shadowed hollows, was no longer merely a quiet heath but a living conduit—an open channel to realms beyond linear time. Every gust of wind carried fragments of distant voices, echoes of a knowledge long suppressed but never entirely silenced. The landscape around him, its subtle shifting, hinted at a presence—evidence of those whose existence preceded history, watchers who had lingered since before the dawn of civilizations, guardians of currents that coursed unseen through the fabric of the universe.

The guardians, as Edith Carrington described them, existed beyond the boundaries of flesh and form—essences composed of pure awareness, shimmering with luminous grace in dimensions that defied human perception. Unlike beings of flesh and blood, they embodied the essence of consciousness itself; their presence felt as a gentle reassurance or a sharp jolt of clarity that sliced through the veil of rational understanding. They operated not through commands or speech but through a shared field of thought—a silent communion that washed over individuals sensitive enough to perceive it. To them, Earth was a sacred node—one among countless spots in a cosmic web—where the currents of time and consciousness crossed in intricate patterns, waiting to be harnessed or disrupted. With eyes closed, Ahmed glimpsed their presence in flashes of iridescent light—like the ripples on a pond disturbed by an unseen force—reminding him that he was beholden to forces older than his understanding, yet intimately tied to his fate.

Throughout the nights that followed, memories of Edith's stories haunted him, their whispers echoing in his mind like spectral melodies. Her narratives painted these guardians as eternal, vigilant, purpose-bound entities—keepers who maintained the delicate balance of the nexus points where the currents of time converge. They served a function far beyond mere observation; they actively preserved the integrity of the temporal streams, intervening subtly whenever the fabric threatened to unravel or fracture. Their purpose was protection—of the planet's hidden pathways, of the spiritual evolution of life embedded in the very structure of reality. Sometimes, Ahmed felt them as an almost tangible presence, threading through the confines of space and time, watching silently, alert to anomalies that might threaten the harmony of existence. These beings, luminous and stately, carried the weight of aeons in their gaze—silent beings whose existence challenged every certitude he carried as a scholar, teasing him with a truth that shimmered just beyond reach, urging him to look deeper, feel more profoundly.

As the night deepened into foreboding quiet, the boundary between the corporeal and the divine blurred. Ahmed's senses sharpened, sensations rippling through him like tremors in a membrane—each breath, each heartbeat synchronizing with the unperceived currents beneath. Somewhere in the dark, an almost imperceptible shift occurred. The air thickened with anticipation. He sensed that these guardians were not distant spectators; they had always been present, woven into the very matter of the earth, waiting for moments when their intervention would be needed. Edith's words echoed in his ears: that the Earth's most sacred spots, like Dorset's deserted deserts and hidden valleys, housed points of convergence—portal sites where the veils between worlds and times grew thinner. These places, she insisted, had been deemed by Lawrence himself as gateways—windows into realms where consciousness could leap beyond its mundane chains and glimpse the infinite.

From the dark, a sudden shimmer pulsed—faint but unmistakable—within the fabric of reality itself. Ahmed's body tensed as he felt a whisper across his mind, an invitation cloaked as a question: would he step through to see what lay beyond, to pierce the illusion that time was fixed and solid? The luminous entities hovered, almost like stars condensed into human forms, their presence both calming and intimidating. They radiated a gentle authority, guardians of epochs and enigma, awaiting the moment when a soul ripe with curiosity and courage would accept the call. Ahmed's rational mind teetered on the edge of surrender and resistance, caught between the intellectual skepticism he once held and a visceral understanding that this was the living truth—an ancient doctrine awakening beneath the surface of his carefully constructed beliefs. The air thrummed with potential, a threshold beckoning on the cusp of something unutterably profound.

Suddenly, a soft glow emanated from the horizon, illuminating the landscape with shifting shades of silver and gold—an otherworldly dawn heralding the next stage of revelation. The guardians' forms blurred into shimmering streams of light, dispersing into the ether as if preparing to reveal a deeper secret. Ahmed's heart hammered against his ribs; his grip on the present loosened as he sensed himself slipping into a state beyond the confines of space and time. In this moment, the boundary dissolved—the guardians' purpose pressing into his consciousness: to balance the delicate currents of evolution, guiding those rare souls capable of perceiving the beyond and navigating its labyrinths. As he stood at the precipice, the echoes of centuries, the hopes of civilizations, and the silent watchfulness of beings beyond comprehension all converged into a single, unfathomable truth—that the descendants of the ancient watchers had always been here, watching, waiting, their purpose entwined with the very fabric of existence, their presence an unwavering testament that some truths lie just beyond the reach of words yet are felt deep within the core of awareness itself.

***

Night had fallen over Bovington Heath, a darkness so thick it seemed to swallow light whole, yet somehow, the air thrummed with an unseen presence. Dr. Ahmed Ridha stood outside the dilapidated cottage, the weight of his recent discoveries pressing upon him like an ancient stone. The sky fractured above—an irregular mosaic of stars smudged across the fabric of space, hinting at something far more complex than mere celestial arrangement. It was as if the universe itself paused, holding its breath in anticipation, waiting for the moment when shadows would yield to truth.

Just beyond his sight, the air shimmered, a flickering ripple that shouldn't have been perceptible but was, in a way that chilled his bones and sparked a flicker of awe. His senses stretched outward, attuned to a presence that transcended form—an awareness that shimmered just beyond the veil of physical reality. These luminous entities, as Edith had described, embodied pure consciousness, their bodies unbound by flesh or bone, crystalline in their simplicity yet infinite in their essence. They radiated a gentle warmth, like dawn breaking across a horizon yet remaining intangible, the very embodiment of awareness itself.

As Ahmed's gaze lifted, the sky seemed to rupture further, revealing a surface that pulsed with iridescent light, shifting between states of solidity and liquid luminescence. He felt rather than saw the beings emerge—tall, luminous figures whose contours flickered in and out of visibility, as if they were made of fragile, shimmering gossamer threaded with eternity. Their presentation was beyond language, beyond thought—an embodiment of the highest form of existence, unencumbered by matter, their essence a pulsating conduit of cosmic knowledge designed to transmit understanding directly into the core of consciousness.

Communication with these beings was not verbal; it was sensation, a sweeping wave of thought that infiltrated his mind with the gentleness of a whisper and the power of a storm. Images flooded him—vast, swirling patterns of energy and light that narrated secrets of a universe unbounded by linear time. They revealed that what humans perceive as solid reality—walls, mountains, even flesh—is merely a temporary veneer, a thin crust on the infinite ocean of consciousness beneath. These luminous entities, guardians of the unseen currents, moved fluidly through the fabric of existence—timeless, formless, and yet profoundly present in every moment of awareness.

He understood suddenly that the barriers he fought to cross—those theoretical boundaries, the scholarly skepticism, the rational scaffolding of his upbringing—were but illusions; the real voyage was into the depths of the self, where the boundaries of form dissolved, revealing an endless expanse of pure being. They showed him visions of Earth's many probabilities, pathways of possible futures unfolding like delicate crochet into the fabric of time—some progressing into spaces of enlightenment, others spiraling into chaos, blinded by forgetfulness of their true nature. The guardian entities, observing with patience, served as silent sentinels and guides, anchoring him in this revelation—reminding him that consciousness was the ultimate creator, the divine architect of worlds both seen and unseen.

In a moment that seemed suspended outside of time, Ahmed's awareness expanded, fitting into the collective consciousness of the luminous beings. He felt himself dissolve into a state beyond self—a deeper, more primal source where all distinctions faded into unity. Colors beyond sight, sounds beyond hearing, and truths unspoken flooded his senses, awakening a knowing that had always been there but long lay dormant beneath the surface of his rational mind. This was no longer the realm of mere scientific hypothesis; it was a living, breathing reality—an infinite dance of possibility that pulsed like a sacred heartbeat. And within that pulse, he sensed the presence of Lawrence, invisible yet unmistakably there, intertwined in the currents of eternity—a reflection of the man who had dared to see beyond the horizon of time, who had glimpsed figures not bound by flesh but by luminous consciousness.

Stars shifted and merged into swirling mosaics, revealing glimpses of worlds where humanity's spiritual evolution had reached transcendence. The luminous entities revealed that Earth was but a node—a nexus point—where these currents intersected most intensely, especially at certain sacred sites. Lawrence had been one such conduit, a human vessel who had ventured into the space where time itself curls and folds—a place Edith called the Sahra Al-Zaman, "The Desert of Time." It was not merely desert nor a physical location, but a state—a suspended awareness accessible to those prepared to surrender the illusions and become custodians of the currents themselves.

As the realization solidified, the entities' presence intensified—an ordered chaos of shimmering photons that spoke directly into the core of his being. Their message was clear: the universe simmers with uncountable potentialities, each a ripple in the vast ocean of consciousness, with humanity poised at a brink of awakening or annihilation. Lawrence's pursuits had not been mere curiosities, but navigational experiments, mapping the uncharted realms where consciousness becomes aware of itself, where linear time unravels and the infinite begins to reveal itself in flashes of crystalline insight. And now, Ahmed found himself woven into this grand design, a new guardian of the currents, a bridge between worlds—silent, luminous, relentless in their divine purpose to guide awareness itself toward its ultimate evolution.

A sudden surge of energy spiraled outward from the beings, spiraling into a kaleidoscope of consciousness that invaded his own with overwhelming clarity. The sensation of merging and diverging, of simultaneous existence across limitless dimensions, threatened to dismantle everything he thought he knew about reality. Yet within that chaos, there was an undeniable harmony—a divine symphony of pure understanding orchestrated by forces far beyond human comprehension. These luminous shapes, these beings of light and void, were neither alive nor dead—they were the architects of existence, caretakers of the threshold where the finite dissolves into the infinite. In that moment, Ahmed knew his role was no longer that of mere scholar, but that of witness, participant, and possibly, co-creator in the ongoing evolution of consciousness.

***

The moment Ahmed stepped beyond the threshold of the dilapidated cottage, an almost imperceptible shift settled over the space. The air itself seemed thicker, weightier with a presence that defied the rational mind's grasp. A gentle hum, not auditory but vibrational—like a resonance rippling through his bones—began to subtly alter his perception. His senses sharpened, not in the typical way, but as if he were attuning to a frequency too delicate for ordinary awareness. It was as though the silence around him concealed a dialogue that transcended words, a conversation transmitted through the very fabric of consciousness itself.

Within the hushed vacuum of his mind, an unspoken exchange unfurled—an influx of images, feelings, and truths that flickered like distant stars across the vault of his awareness. He sensed the consciousnesses from beyond linear time, beings whose existence was woven into the very currents of the universe, communicating not through sound but through pure intent. These entities, luminous and fluid, conveyed understanding directly—an effortless flow of knowledge that bypassed language, shape-shifting into emotive waves that washed over him with the gentleness of a whisper yet the intensity of revelation. His own consciousness responded instinctively, connecting him to these unseen currents, as if awakening from a deep, collective slumber.

Extending outward, the boundaries of his self dissolved—no longer confined to the physical body or the limitations of thought. Instead, he became part of a vast, shimmering web of awareness, where each node pulsed with encrypted symbolism and silent messages. He felt them—others who had glimpsed this space before, guardians or explorers of the unseen pathways. Their presence shared a luminous patience, encouraging him, inviting him to glimpse a truth that had long been hidden behind guarded veils of linear perception. Here, in the stillness, communication was a symphony of consciousness, played in silence yet resonating with profound clarity, beyond words or interference—the universal language of awareness itself.

His mind, now a vessel open to this ether, experienced a cascade of impressions—visions of ancient civilizations, echoes of cosmic architectures, strange geometries that defied Euclidean logic. These visions conveyed that the universe was a living, breathing consciousness—an endless lattice of currents, folds, and flows—whose communications shimmered in the spaces between moments. As the entities' presence washed over him, the boundaries between observer and observed blurred, and Ahmed understood that this transmission had little to do with decoding messages but rather about aligning with a higher frequency—where thought, emotion, and intention became inertial points of a greater, shared consciousness. It was here, in this silent exchange, that the deepest truths resided, waiting patiently for those willing to listen beneath the noise of the surface world.

Gradually, the wave of energy subsided, yet the sense of connection persisted—an indelible imprint woven into his mind's fabric. For a moment, he perceived the universe's vast chatter as a gentle muse, whispering secrets into the quiet corners of his being. The realization dawned that such exchanges were not fraught with mere data or superficial signals, but rather a transmission of intent—an act of consciousness itself sending and receiving information as naturally as breath. This silent dialogue beckoned him—an invitation to transcend limitations, to inhabit a state where words became redundant and understanding blossomed instantaneously. The mastery of this form of communication, he sensed, was integral to the evolution of human awareness—an awakening that would unlock the potential for higher states of being, where worlds beyond sight and sound convened in an eternal, unspoken symphony.

As the luminous entities withdrew into the depths of the cosmic expanse, a lingering resonance flickered within Ahmed—an echo of something profound yet ineffably simple. It was the understanding that the universe communicated constantly, whether through the rustling leaves or the silent pulse of the celestial bodies; that in the stillness of the night or in the breath before dawn, the highest truths were offered freely, waiting to be embraced by those open enough to perceive their language. In that moment, acknowledgment dawned—the realization that the entire cosmos was a vast, interconnected consciousness, whispering its secrets in the language of silence, accessible only to those who dared to listen beyond the clamor of surface reality. This recognition set into motion the first flicker of a new understanding: consciousness was not merely a property of beings but the foundation of existence itself, and communication in this realm occurred through the delicate currents of awareness—a dance of energetic exchange woven deeply into the fabric of all that is and ever will be.

***

Nine
The Infinite Ocean
Time as a Liquid Realm

Ahmed sat behind the wheel of his battered car, the engine's sputtering cough echoing through the sprawling Dorset heathland as twilight dissolved into a veil of indigo. The landscape around him had shifted from familiar to uncanny, each twisted branch and shadowed hill whispering stories beyond rational comprehension. The crash had been sudden, a jagged rupture in his journey—an interruption that felt less like mechanical failure and more like a tie severed from a deeper, unseen fabric. As he stepped out into the cool evening air, the air itself seemed thick with anticipation, as if the very earth was holding its breath, waiting for something to emerge from the shifting depths of possibility.

The sky above fractured suddenly, not with storm or wind but with a subtle tremor—an almost imperceptible ripple that coursed across the fabric of reality, stirring the leaves and causing the clouds to flicker like candle flames caught in a gentle disturb. Ahmed's gaze lifted involuntarily, sensing the currents of time swirling in ripples across the horizon. His conscious mind, trained in skepticism, struggled to reconcile the surreal beauty unfolding before him with his logical paradigm; yet, beneath his rational surface, a flicker of curiosity ignited, whispering that these disturbances were no accident but signals—signs of the currents that carve the invisible contours of possibility. The universe, he now understood, was an ocean of liquid time, each ripple carrying potential realities, each wave a vessel of shifting destinies.

He remembered Edith's words, her voice weaving through the hazy evening like a prayer—speaking of currents that flow beneath the surface of what can be seen, carrying us toward moments of decision, transformation, or chaos. Her stories had spoken of Lawrence's investigations into these very phenomena—hidden within the sands of Arabia and the quiet corners of Dorset, where the land itself listened for the whispers of non-linear time. Now, standing on the verge of something unknown, Ahmed felt the certainty that these ripples were more than mere atmospheric anomalies. They were the echoes of possibilities waiting to be navigated, like unseen streams diverging and converging in a vast, turbulent ocean, each choice sending ripples of influence through the fabric of reality.

The dimming twilight cast shadows that flickered between the real and the imagined, as if the boundary between worlds was thinning to a whisper. Ahead, the landscape seemed to ripple—distorting in places, revealing glimpses of what lay beneath the surface of space and time. His skin prickled with a strange sensation—a faint pulse, like the heartbeat of a universe that breathes and shifts. He stepped forward, each footfall imprinting tiny disturbances in the soil, creating ripples that spread outward into the darkness. He was beginning to understand that this moment was a junction—a gateway where awareness could choose which currents to follow, where possibilities could multiply or converge into one point of certainty. This was the nexus of potential, the epicenter of the flow that moved all things and none at once.

Suddenly, the horizon fractured entirely, like glass shattering in slow motion, revealing a sliver of shimmering light—an iridescent ripple cutting through the night, expanding with silent grace. From this, a wave of energy emanated, coursing through the air, bending and twisting the very fabric of his perception. It was a living substance, this ripple, inviting him to step into its flow—to become a navigator in the vast, liquid realm of possibility. The currents inside him stirred—fears and hopes commingling—yet beneath the turbulence, something ancient and profound whispered that movement across these ripples was not random but purposeful. There was an order, a melody tuned to the frequencies of consciousness itself, waiting to be tuned into. He sensed that the universe's endless dance—the undulating waves and swirling eddies—held the key not just to understanding the world but to shaping its unfolding narrative.

Closing his eyes for a moment, Ahmed felt the vision expand beyond his senses, a subtle oscillation swaying across the layers of reality, drawing him into a realm where the distinction between past, present, and future blurred into a shimmering continuum. The ripples, he understood now, were like the strokes of a cosmic painter—each wave a brushstroke that could alter the entire canvas of existence. His awareness became a vessel, riding the undulations without resistance, guided by an intuitive sense of direction. At that instant, a thought surfaced—an insight that time was not a rigid river flowing in one direction but a vast liquid that one could learn to navigate. Every decision, every moment of focus influenced the currents, creating new ripples—new pathways—leading into futures yet unseen. The flow was not fixed but a tapestry of floating opportunities, waiting for consciousness to steer its course.

As the ripples continued to pulse outward like gentle surges, Ahmed's mind opened to the silent symphony of possibilities. He saw his own choices reflected in the shifting pattern of waves—each one a potential crossing of thresholds, each ripple an invitation to diverge or converge. The thought made his skin tingle as though a new sensory door had opened—one that allowed him to perceive time's liquid essence. And in that moment, he realized that the currents beneath the surface were not just natural phenomena but consciously navigable channels—a navigational map made of thought, intention, and memory. Just as a sailor reads the ripples to steer through unpredictable waters, so too must he learn to attune himself to these unseen streams. This was the true mastery—the art of sensing the currents of potential and moving with them, rather than against them.

And so, with his heart pounding in rhythm with the undulating waves of possibility, Ahmed took a tentative step forward into the darkness. The landscape around him was no longer solely a physical territory but a living, breathing ocean of infinite possibilities that called for awareness and courage. Each ripple that crested before him carried whispers of worlds that could be—the futures shaped by consciousness, the past woven into the present like threads of a divine loom. His mind, unmoored yet focused, began to trace the paths that these ripples offered, knowing that in riding the flows of this liquid realm, he was not merely observing but participating in the greatest act of creation—navigating the currents that connect all moments, all selves, all worlds. The flow of possibility was alight with promise—and the choice to follow was his alone to make.

***

Ahmed's fingers trembled slightly as he sat beside Edith's worn leather armchair, the dim glow of the oil lamp casting elongated shadows across the cluttered interior of the bungalow. The air was thick with the scent of ancient paper, roasted tea leaves, and something indefinably ancient—an echo of worlds long passed, or perhaps those yet to come. Outside, the Dorset night pressed against the windows, but within this space, a silence seemed to pulse with the heartbeat of unseen currents. He had entered something that defied logic, stepping through a threshold he had scarcely understood, and now, the very fabric of linear time felt like molten glass, ready to shatter at the slightest touch.

Edith's voice, husky yet resonant, broke the stillness. She wove stories of Lawrence's clandestine pursuits—not merely military stratagems or desert adventures but strange experiments that blurred the boundaries between worlds, between what was and what could be. Her words painted pictures of Lawrence pacing before flickering firelight, reciting verses from the Quran in perfect Arabic, his voice rising and falling within the confines of the room, as Sassoon's scribbles and Augustus John's sketches materialized from the ether. The stories seemed to ripple through the air, their texture thick with the scent of sandalwood and dust, a reminder that history was not fixed but malleable, fluid as the sea.

As she revealed Lawrence's journals—authentic, undeniable—the pages came alive beneath Ahmed's gaze. The handwriting itself seemed to shimmer with an internal light, each stroke a portal into a mind obsessed not with victory but with understanding that the tides of time could be shifted, bent, manipulated. Lawrence's detailed notes spoke of chronological displacement events, phenomena that fractured the linear march of history and hinted at the existence of locations across the globe—places where the walls of time dissolved, revealing glimpses of higher planes. The sketches, abstract yet unmistakably crafted with intent, depicted craft that defied aerodynamic constraints, vessels that shimmered between matter and energy, hovering on the brink of perception.

Edith leaned forward, her eyes luminous with unspoken knowledge. Her voice lowered into a whisper as she deciphered Lawrence's cryptic dedication "To S.A.," revealing it as an abbreviation not for a person but for Sahra Al-Zaman, the Desert of Time. Her words unfurled like sacred parchment—Lawrence had discovered that certain terrains and spaces on Earth served as gateways to the universe's hidden flow. These were not mere geographical features but nodes in an intricate, invisible map of temporal currents. The desert, she explained, was a living entity—an abyss where time's malleability was laid bare for those who possessed the insight to perceive it. Here, amid the shifting sands, Lawrence had glimpsed the truth that reality was a spectrum, a universe of possibilities, not a single, unbendable thread.

The night deepened, and Edith's stories took on a strange, otherworldly intensity. Her voice grew softer yet more urgent as she described her own role as one of the custodians of this realm—a guardian of one of the many temporal nexuses. She spoke of luminous beings, entities not confined to flesh but existing as consciousness, watching over the passages that link different moments in time and space. Their listening presence suggested a vast, silent council, observing humanity's evolution from afar while subtly nudging its course. Ahmed, caught in the rising tide of her revelations, felt his rational mind unraveling. He had thought himself a scholar, a seeker of facts, yet now the universe whispered that some truths lay beyond the grasp of empirical certainty, embedded within the folds of consciousness itself.

Then, just as dawn threatened the horizon, the air shifted—an electric pulse passing through the room, incrementally crescendoing until it became a resonant hum in Ahmed's ears. Edith's eyes sparkled with a rare fire.

"It's almost time," she murmured, glancing at the ancient clock on the mantle. *"Lawrence's hour.* The moment when he would depart into that thin space between worlds, when the currents aligned to reveal what lay hidden beneath the surface of existence."

Ahmed froze as a profound silence enveloped everything; a stillness that was heavier, thicker than any sound, yet vibrated with the sensation of unseen wings fluttering just beyond perception. Outside, the sky above Clouds Hill fractured as if lent from an ancient manuscript—torn edges curling inward, revealing a shimmer that defied shape. The stars fragmented into a shimmering mosaic, casting fractured light that pulsed in sync with his own heartbeat. Even the ground beneath him seemed to breathe, as if the very earth remembered that it was woven into a liquid fabric of time, flowing like a vast, cosmic sea.

Suddenly, a luminous presence emerged from the fractured sky—tall, shimmering forms that carried no weight in sight but radiated a knowledge so ancient it seemed to pulse through Ahmed's consciousness. They moved through dimensions, flickering between solid and intangible, their forms echoing evolution beyond human form. Their thoughts, resonant and direct, coursed into his mind in a multitude of tongues—Arabic, English, and whispers of a language predating speech itself. They conveyed a message of purpose: guardians of consciousness, stewards of a universe that was fundamentally liquid, malleable, stretching across unseen currents. To them, Earth was on the verge of a crucial moment—an intersection where human awareness must choose whether to navigate the infinite or fall back into the confines of the linear, limited story of existence.

Ahmed sensed that his own identity was dissolving in this vast ocean of awareness, his boundaries melting into the stream of higher consciousness that enveloped him. The beings showed him visions of countless possibilities—timelines where humanity blossomed into cosmic awareness, and others where it self-destructed in blindness. The choice, they implied, lay in the awareness of the currents, in recognizing the cognitive fluidity of time and space—an act of conscious participation in the universe's unfolding. The realization struck him deeply: Time was not a river but a liquid expanse, shifting in waves and ripples, with each individual acting as an unconscious vessel navigating its flowing depths.

When Ahmed's senses returned, the metaphysical tide subsided, leaving him in the quiet ruins of the cottage. The ancient walls, once broken and buried beneath decades of neglect, now seemed to ripple with a muted energy, as if they carried the whispers of the beings who had traversed those currents before him. Carefully, he uncovered artifacts—Lawrence's maps marked with symbols unlike any known language, inscriptions of profound wisdom, and a typewritten note in Lawrence's own hand, inscribed with flowing Arabic script: "Find Sahra Al-Zaman." It was not a place but a state of consciousness—a realm entirely accessible to those who understood the liquid fabric of time.

In the shadowed corner of the room, amid the layered debris of years, Ahmed uncovered something startling: a crystalline device, its facets shimmering with undiscovered light. The object seemed to hum with a residual frequency, resonating with the cosmic currents Lawrence once studied. The discovery was more than an artifact—it was a key, a fragment of that fluid universe, promising entry into the next phase of human evolution. Yet more compelling than the object itself was the sense of a mission; a purpose infused with the whisperings of those beyond the linear, beckoning him into a realm where past, present, and future dissolved into pure awareness. Ahmed realized, in that instant, he was no longer merely a historian—he was becoming a guardian, a traveler on the liquid ocean of time, tasked with guiding others toward the realization of their cosmic potential.

***

The night settled heavily over Bovington Heath, an oppressive silence wrapping the landscape like a shroud, broken only by the faint whisper of drifting wind and the distant cry of a fox. Lawrence's memory lingered in the air, its ghostly presence woven into the very fabric of the earth beneath Ahmed's trembling feet. As he stepped outside the rambling bungalow—its irregular walls faintly shimmering in the moonlight—an inexplicable pull tugged at his consciousness, as if unseen hands were beckoning him toward the horizon's edge. Every shadow seemed alive, shifting subtly, hinting at a realm where the bounds of time and space blurred into a liquid, flowing tapestry. A sense of anticipation coursed through him, thickening with the weight of the unseen forces awakening around him, forces that understood the language of luminosity and silence more than words ever could.

Within the profound darkness, the sky suddenly fractured like fractured ancient parchment, revealing impossible shapes—mysterious crafts that defied known physics—hovering just beyond comprehension. Their surfaces reflected starlight and liquid fire, shifting between metal and light in a dance that seemed both elegant and ominous. From the ether, beings emerged—tall, luminous figures that shimmered with a consciousness far beyond human cognition. Their forms suggested evolution past biology, a state of pure awareness spun into corporeal manifestation, their presence pulsing with a gentle rhythm that resonated directly within Ahmed's mind. These entities communicated, not through sound, but through a wave of thought that flowed seamlessly into his consciousness, filling every corner of his awareness with images, scents, and feelings beyond language's reach. They spoke of cosmic thresholds, of Earth's silent acknowledgment as a nexus point where awareness unfurled into infinite dimensions, and

Ahmad's role as a bridge between this world and the unseen was not accidental but primordial.

As the beings revealed their purpose—guardians of these intersections, custodians of consciousness—Ahmed descended into a whirlpool of realization. He saw in his mind's eye the earth's many probability streams, pathways branching into futures of both enlightenment and chaos, depending on whether humanity listened or ignored the signals whispering through the fabric of reality. These guardians knew the delicate art of navigating the liquid currents of time, of slipping fluidly from one possibility to another, and in that moment, Ahmed understood that Lawrence's retreat to Clouds Hill, once dismissed by scholars as mere refuge, was in fact a carefully concealed act—an act of exploration into the very nature of time itself. Lawrence had been investigating the malleable fabric of the cosmos, charting unseen currents that seemed to ripple beneath the surface of history. His dedication, Edith confided, was rooted in the knowledge that certain locations held the keys to unlock the fluidity of time—a realization that transformed Lawrence from a mere soldier in the desert into a pilgrim seeking the eternal.

Suddenly, a surge of harmonic resonance—felt rather than heard—spiraled upward from the horizon, a symphony woven from the threads of existence itself. Ahmed's senses expanded beyond the physical, no longer bounded by his body's limitations. The craft above shimmered brighter, its surface becoming a shifting mosaic of liquid light, revealing glimpses of higher realms—worlds where consciousness thrived in perpetual becoming, unbound by linearity. The luminous beings extended their awareness into him, sharing visions of Earth's multiple probable futures: one of ascension, bathed in cosmic consciousness, and another of self-destruction rooted in denial of the infinite. Their message was clear—humanity's spiritual evolution was awakening on the threshold of a great shift, and Lawrence's true purpose had been to prepare the ground, to act as a conduit for these forces that transcended history's narrow confines. In that luminous space, Ahmed perceived his own destiny—a moment where past, present, and future coalesced into an endless flow, a liquid universe where possibilities ripple like waves across an infinite ocean, beckoning him to choose his course amid the chaos and stillness.

When the visions subsided and the entities dissolved back into the ether, Ahmed found himself alone again—standing amidst the remnants of the old cottage, its walls now silent and seemingly woven into the fabric of the dawn's early light. In his trembling hand, he clutched a crystalline object the beings had left behind—a fragment not of this world, yet undeniably real, pulsing softly with a luminous heartbeat. As the first pale rays of sunlight pierced the horizon, he turned slowly, sensing that this object was more than a mere artifact; it was a portal, a key to the unseen currents he was now charged to navigate. His mind raced to reconcile what had happened—an encounter that blurred the boundaries between science and mysticism, history and eternity—yet the truth was in his bones: Lawrence's legacies stretched far beyond the confines of mundane history. The true mission now became clear. Like those luminous guardians, he was to serve as a keeper of the thresholds, a conduit for the awakening of consciousness that would ripple across timelines and dimensions—the destined point where humanity must confront the liquid ocean of time itself, and either sink into its depths or rise from it, transformed forever.

***

Ten

Consciousness as the Prime Creative Force

The night hung heavy over Bovington Heath, a silence that pressed upon Ahmed like an ancient weight, yet within it pulsated a subtle hum—an inaudible vibration that seemed to emanate from the very fabric of causality itself. The world outside had dimmed into shadow, and the only illumination came from the faint flicker of the cottage's windows, casting long, tortuous shadows that danced with every shifting gust of wind. Ahmed stood at the threshold of what he had believed to be merely an abandoned relic, but now he sensed its dimension had shifted, become something more—an intersection point for that restless, intangible energy which he could feel thrumming in his veins. His mind raced, caught between skepticism and the flickering whisper of possibility, as he endeavored to grasp the unfathomable power threaded through every thought—each idea, each memory, a ripple capable of shaping worlds yet unseen.

Inside, the air shimmered with a palpable tension; objects—not merely inanimate artifacts but vessels of consciousness—seemed to vibrate with unspoken knowledge. The dusty volumes of Lawrence's journals, the delicate Persian miniatures, and the relics of an era long past glowed faintly, as if awakened by the very presence of Ahmed's questions. His thoughts whirled around the idea that thought itself was a malleable substance—not a mere epiphenomenon of brain activity but a force capable of bending reality. It was as if each whisper of doubt or hope carved pathways in the cosmic tapestry, nudging the universe toward potentialities. Every mental image he conjured, every inkling of curiosity, appeared to resonate outward, subtly altering the shadows and shapes that cloaked the room, whispering that consciousness was no passive mirror but an active shaper of existence.

Edith's words echoed in his mind—stories of Lawrence reciting Quranic verses with precision or Sassoon scribbling feverish notes while contemplating a future submerged in unseen currents of time. Their images flickered, momentarily alive, as if the very essence of their awareness still lingered, waiting to be invoked by focused intent. Edith's voice, gentle yet commanding, had spoken of the desert as a realm of infinite possibility—where the sands stretched beyond the limits of linear time, where past, present, and future blurred into a single, malleable thread. Ahmed felt a stirring deep within, a visceral sense that thought—the act of pure intention—could be a key capable of unlocking this concealed domain. That every notion held the potential to manifest worlds, to influence currents of unseen energy that wove through the fabric of eternity, was an idea poised on the brink of becoming truth.

The creeping dawn cast a pallid light through the cracked windows, illuminating dust motes dancing like tiny spirits suspended in the unseen ether. As the first rays pierced the gloom, Ahmed's awareness shifted—an almost imperceptible movement that rippled through his core, stirring a new understanding. He perceived himself no longer as a mere observer of history or a seeker of hidden truths but as an active participant in the ongoing dialogue between consciousness and reality. The moment he embraced the malleability of thought—realizing that each desire, each question, each faint hope was a seed capable of blossoming into tangible manifestation—the very essence of his purpose seemed to crackle into existence. Time itself felt less like a fixed corridor and more like a fluid, mutable ocean, waiting to respond to the currents of intent he could begin to direct. It became increasingly clear that the universe was built upon this energetic dance—thoughts sending tendrils into the void, pulling from the depths possibilities yet unseen.

Standing amidst relics and shadows, Ahmed's breath quickened as a surge of clarity rippled through his consciousness—an understanding that his mind, often considered a vessel for rationality, could instead serve as an architect of realities. It was no longer an abstract notion but an active process; every mental act, a deliberate imprint pressing into the fabric of the cosmos. This insight sparked an immediate, visceral sensation—the knowledge that the universe responded to intention, that focused thought could bend the patterns of space and time. The realization carried with it both awe and responsibility, for with this power came the understanding that illusion and reality were intertwined by invisible threads woven from subtle energies. The malleability of perception, of belief, was the key to the true creative force, and Ahmed's awakening was only just beginning, teetering on the edge of this powerful truth—a truth that promised liberation from the linear chains of ordinary existence.

The night seemed to hold its breath as the boundary between the known and unknown continued to dissolve, revealing glimpses of a universe where thought defined form, where consciousness was the architect of all that was, and all that could be. Ahmed's fingers trembled as he reached toward a worn leather-bound volume, feeling the weight of centuries of silent potential embedded within its pages. His mind aligned with the silent principle that every act of thinking could ripple outward, manifesting into waves that touched across dimensions—if only one knew how to consciously steer this energy. The oppressive weight of skepticism, the rigidity of academic logic, all teetered as the unspoken power of intention unfurled within him. He saw, with startling clarity, that every moment of doubt, every flicker of hope, could be catalysts—small sparks igniting the vast, undefined landscape of possibility. The universe responded, responsive to the nuanced cadence of his thought, inviting him into a dance where he was both creator and recipient of the universe's deepest truths.

As the first light of dawn spilled across the heath, Ahmed's sense of self dissolved into a profound awareness: consciousness was the seed from which reality blossomed, the primordial energy that shaped matter and mind alike. This was the revelation that had eluded him in academic halls—an understanding that the universe was not separate from the mind, but constructed from its very patterns. Each idea, each flicker of intention, could carve new pathways through the silent currents, reweaving the web of existence itself. The power was in his grasp, subtle yet immense—a whisper away from becoming a roar. The knowing settled within him like the slow deep breath of the earth awakening, filling his entire being with the weightlessness of possibility. The universe, in its quiet way, responded to the malleability of thought, and Ahmed sensed that he stood at the threshold of this ancient, infinite dance—ready now to co-create, to manifest beyond the constraints that had long bound human perception.

***

The evening shadows grew darker as Ahmed stepped closer to Clouds Hill, the faint amber glow of the setting sun casting elongated silhouettes across the sprawling Dorset heath. The landscape seemed to breathe softly—each pebble and patch of moss whispering secrets older than memory, as if the land itself conspired to unveil unseen truths. His engine had sputtered and died, leaving him stranded at the brink of an ancient threshold, where the boundary between the familiar and the unknown blurred with an almost palpable tension. The air hung heavy with the scent of damp earth and hidden potentials, stirring a restless anticipation as night tiptoed into the horizon. Something about this place—its silence, its stillness—felt charged, alive with the echo of voices from other times and dimensions.

As he lifted his gaze, a figure appeared on the porch, moving with an effortless grace that seemed to transcend the confines of ordinary motion. Lady Edith Currington—elegant, poised, and radiating a quiet authority—arose from her seat. She carried herself as if she belonged to a world beyond the mundane, her eyes reflecting depths that beckoned rather than warned. Her voice, when she spoke, was composed yet imbued with an almost hypnotic melody, as if holding keys to ancient chambers of consciousness. She welcomed Ahmed as an old friend summoned by fate, her presence subtly shifting the space between skepticism and longing. In that instant, the boundary between scholar and mystic dissolved, leaving only a shared curiosity tethered to the infinite horizon ahead.

The interior was a portal in itself—walls adorned with a silent symphony of relics, manuscripts, and artifacts that seemed to pulse with life. Every shelf held silent witnesses: first editions of Burton's Arabian Nights nestled beside forgotten scrolls of Doughty's Arabia Deserta, Persian miniatures casting shimmering reflections on the wood panels. Bedouin silver, delicate yet primal, hung as if caught mid-moment between the earthy and the divine. The scent of aged paper and lacquered wood mingled with a gentle hum of unseen energy, suggesting that within these walls, history was not merely stored but alive, whispering its eternal stories. Lady Edith poured tea—a dark, fragrant pu-erh long deemed lost to time—and offered it with a reverence that hinted at a deeper purpose. As Ahmed hesitated, she smiled softly, her every gesture suggesting that this convergence was no accident but a destined crossing.

Then came the stories—unfolding like delicate tapestries woven from shadow and light. Edith described nights when Lawrence would pace before the fireplace, reciting verses of the Quran in flawless Arabic, his voice a vessel transmitting something beyond words. Sassoon, scribbling furiously, had captured that strange rhythm as if transcribing the resonance of another realm. Augustus John's sketches depicted not only the man but the restless energy that seemed to ripple around him, a hint of veiled knowledge yearning to emerge. Edith's voice softened further as she narrated Lawrence's late-night debates with Nancy Astor, fierce dialogues about the future of the Arab world that continued until dawn, each exchange an echo of a deeper, perhaps unseen, reality. The very fabric of those stories challenged Ahmed—what he credited as history was only a fragment, a mask hiding the greater truths Lawrence had sought beneath layers of myth and conquest.

What truly transformed the moment was Edith's mention of Lawrence's retreat to Clouds Hill—not as mere refuge but as a gateway into the corridors of time itself. She spoke of her own childhood, of strange phenomena that punctuated Dorset's quiet landscapes: shimmering lights dancing at the edge of perception, subtle distortions in the air, and whispers carried on the wind that seemed to echo from other eras. Her words insinuated that Lawrence's fascination extended beyond the geopolitical—he had glimpsed portals, the very fabric of the earth woven with threads of temporal energy. This revelation lurked at the fringes of Ahmed's rational mind, tugging insistently at the borders of skepticism, hinting at a universe far stranger and more interconnected than any map or scholarly model could suggest.

The turning point arrived when Edith produced Lawrence's journals—delicately bound volumes, each page alive with the pulsating ink of someone who had dared to record what was forbidden. The handwriting, unmistakably his, told of meticulous observations not only of military campaigns but of phenomena that defied conventional physics. Descriptions of "chronological displacement events," as he called them, detailed moments where time shimmered, split, or reversed—visions of a universe where causality was but a suggestion, a fleeting illusion woven into the grander continuum. Sketches of inexplicable craft, shimmering with impossible geometries, hinted at craft that had no place in the known history of aviation or technology. Ahmed's grasp of the world was loosening; these pages revealed a mind that had been on the verge of understanding a truth beyond the veil of linearity, yet never dared fully to breach it.

Most startling was Edith's assertion that Lawrence's dedication "To S.A." in *Seven Pillars of Wisdom* was a secret salute—an acknowledgment not of a person, but of "Sahra Al-Zaman," the Desert of Time. According to her, Lawrence had uncovered that certain locations act as nodes—points where the currents of time and consciousness intersect. The barren sands of the Arabian Peninsula, the silent expanse of Dorset, the depths of the desert—each held a connection to a greater, invisible grid running across space and history itself. These nexus points, Edith explained, were anchors in the cosmic web—places where reality's fabric could be tugged and reshaped by those who understood the language of these currents. The implications were staggering: the desert was not merely a vast empty space but a stage for phenomena that pierced the fabric of existence itself, revealing that time was an ocean capable of flowing in many directions simultaneously.

By night's deepening hush, Edith's voice grew softer, yet more intense. She revealed herself as a guardian of one such nexus—a keeper whose silent vigil spanned decades. Her stories intertwined her own memories with those of Lawrence's clandestine investigations into the unseen—visions of beings from beyond linear perception, guardians of consciousness evolution who monitored humanity's progress since the dawn of existence. These beings, she said, communicated not through words but through consciousness itself—thoughts transmitted across impossible distances, aligning with the very core of human awareness. For Ahmed, the boundary between the known and the mysterious dissolved, revealing a universe where spirits and matter, time and eternity exist in perpetual communion—where mastery of the mind meant access to the infinite.

The climax approached as the hour struck—precisely 3:17 AM—what Edith called "Lawrence's hour," when the earth and sky seemed to shudder at the threshold of shifts unseen. Ahmed felt a resonant hum, a frequency pulsing through his bones, summoning him outside into the darkness. Above, the sky fractured like ancient parchment, revealing a craft of crystalline beauty suspended in the cosmic void—a symphony of shimmering light and liquid metals, shifting and flowing across multiple states of existence. From the depths of that celestial portal emerged luminous entities, radiating brilliance, shifting forms beyond human words or comprehension. These beings, towering and silent, embodied pure consciousness—evolving, unfolding, eternal. Their minds brushed against Ahmed's, transmitting visions of worlds within worlds and lessons of power and responsibility.

They revealed that Earth's unfolding future was a tapestry of countless probabilities—some luminous, others perilous. Ahmed saw glimpses of a human race awakening to its own divine potential, capable of transcending the illusion of separation and entering realms of profound unity. Yet darker timelines lurked, where neglect of the invisible currents led to chaos and self-destruction. The beings told him that consciousness was the primal creative force, a truth long known to mystics and visionaries—those who could navigate the currents of time and space. These pathways, they explained, belonged to individuals endowed with the rare ability to unify the fragmented perceptions of reality, guiding others toward the resurrection of the true self beyond the masks of history and myth. And as Ahmed gazed into this infinite ocean, he understood that his journey was no longer confined to scholarly inquiry but part of a larger awakening—one that would demand courage and insight to carry into a future suffused with unseen wonders.

***

The dusk hung heavily over Bovington Heath, a murky curtain drawn across the wide, windswept expanse where the heather and gorse seemed to breathe in the cold, relentless air. Ahmed's hands trembled slightly on the steering wheel as mechanical failure whispered its final protest, the vehicle's engine sputtering into silence with a sudden, mournful gasp. The landscape stretched emptily around him, a silent witness to an unfolding rite—one that would fracture the thin veneer of his rational existence. Shadows lengthened, and the sky above fractured into jagged slivers of light, as if the universe itself were cracking open at the seams, revealing something deeper pulsing beyond comprehension.

In the ominous silence, Ahmed stepped out, the chill of the coming night seeping into his bones. His gaze darted across the undulating terrain, spotting the familiar shape of Clouds Hill in the distance—yet what awaited him bore no resemblance to the sanctuary he'd known from countless photographs. Instead, nestled among twisted pale trees and under the weight of sprawling rhododendrons, a rambling bungalow materialized, its architectural lines suggesting a history older than the war-torn image preserved in books or famed in legend. Warm amber light spilled from its windows, casting inviting pools onto the darkened earth, and from the porch, an elderly woman sat poised with an air of effortless grace, her figure radiating authority and serenity without pretense—Lady Edith Carrington, her presence enough to stir a hush within the wind itself.

The inside of the bungalow defied any modest expectations. Walls lined with shelves bore stacks of first editions—Burton's Arabian Nights sharing space with Doughty's Arabia Deserta—while Persian miniatures and silver filigree from Bedouin tribes adorned every corner. The air carried the faint aroma of cardamom, ancient ink, and something more elusive—an essence of history itself, as if the very walls pulsed with stories waiting patiently in silence. Edith poured a delicate, fragrant pu-erh tea into fine porcelain cups, retaining a practiced elegance. Her voice, when she finally spoke, was a gentle yet commanding melody, as if music and memory intertwined seamlessly, drawing Ahmed into a dialogue that felt both intimate and eternal. She detailed her longstanding familiarity with the landscape's secret energies, describing moments of presence that transcended the physical, whispering of what Lawrence once suspected but had dared not speak aloud: the land's hidden gateways to realms beyond time.

As the night thickened, Edith's stories painted Lawrence not simply as a foreign officer or a daring adventurer, but as something far more profound. She spoke of his midnight pacing, reciting Quranic verses with fierce clarity, of Sassoon scribbling frenzied notes as Lawrence's restless translations fluttered from his lips like sparks in the dark. Debates with Edith's own contemporaries—Nancy Astor, Augustus John—became vivid scenes upon the hearth, heated with the energy of minds converging on truths too vast for language. Yet amid these vivid memories, Edith's tone grew increasingly cryptic. She revealed that Lawrence's sojourn to Clouds Hill was less about retreat and more about seeking portals—an exploration into the fabric where history and myth converged. Her words hinted at phenomena that bore the hallmarks of the extraordinary: temporal anomalies that had haunted her youth, flickering signatures on the edges of perception, like the universe itself hinting at a secret it was willing to share only with those prepared to see beyond.

Ahmed's skepticism wavered as Edith unsealed a bound leather volume—Lawrence's own journals, long believed lost in the chaos of 1919. The handwriting was unmistakable, each letter infused with an eager, almost frantic energy. The entries bore scientific precision—accounts of "displacement events," "chronological shifts" witnessed during desert campaigns, sketches of flying craft that defied any known aerodynamic principles. These pages hinted at a mind not merely engaged with strategy but delving into unknown dimensions of consciousness—visions that transcended linear time and inhabited a space beyond logic's grasp. Ahmed's breath caught as he studied the detailed diagrams of what appeared to be vehicles—a hybrid of myth and machinery—rendered with an almost mystical intent. He questioned aloud, the words uncertain, whether these were mere fantasies or something more tangible, but Edith's calm eyes held no doubt—these were gateways, and Lawrence had been among their explorers.

Then Edith's voice turned darker, revealing the true enigma behind Lawrence's enigmatic dedication, "To S.A." Her lips brushed the phrase like a secret, revealing that it referred not to individual names but to something profound—"Sahra Al-Zaman," the "Desert of Time." She explained that Lawrence's pursuits extended into the realm of metaphysics, discovering that certain Earth locations stood at intersections—crucial nodes where time's fabric thinned and the currents of possibility fluctuated wildly. These spots, she believed, were the real focus of Lawrence's deepest experiments; their potential to bend reality had driven him into the shadows, seeking forces that mankind was scarcely prepared to understand. The realization hung in the air as shadows stretched long across the worn wooden floors, thick with the weight of her words, a promise of worlds hidden just beyond the veil of perception.

Gradually, the room grew imbued with an otherworldly aura. Edith's tone shifted into a hushed reverence—she confessed her own custodial role, guarding one such nexus. She detailed beings that transcended physicality—luminous entities whose forms shimmered with evolution, consciousness that radiated beyond form itself. Their communication was a silent symphony—thoughts transmitted through shared awareness, passing across dimensions like the ripples on a still pond. These entities, she explained, had been monitoring Earth's evolution for countless centuries, studying the human journey as part of a grand cosmic mosaic. For them, Lawrence's quest was not merely about conquest or adventure; it was a conscious effort to catalyze humanity's leap into higher states of awareness. The air grew heavier, charged with the electric promise that these forces, unseen yet felt, were preparing to converge, with Ahmed now cast as an unwitting participant in a process centuries in the making.

The night blurred into moments—moments that seemed to stretch and fold within themselves—until, at precisely 3:17 AM, the air thickened with a resonance that could only be described as a symphony of vibrations. Edith, eyes shimmering with a mixture of awe and calm, called it "Lawrence's hour"—the moment when the old cyclist would ride into the unseen, chasing whispers of eternity. Ahmed was compelled forward, his feet moving instinctively as he stepped outside, where the darkness felt thick and alive. Above the cottage, the sky fractured visually—an antique parchment torn and reassembled in impossible geometries—revealing a craft of woven light and metal, shifting seamlessly across multiple states of existence. Its surface flickered like a mirror, a liquid tableau of alien beauty, suggesting dimensions where matter and energy dissolved into pure consciousness. A feeling of raw presence filled the air—timeless, vast, and intimately personal.

From this craft emerged beings unlike any Ahmed had encountered in his quiet, rational world—tall, luminous forms that seemed to breathe with the universe itself, their entity shimmering with wisdom far exceeding human understanding. They communicated through thought—complex, layered, laden with meaning—flowing directly into his mind in languages that did not merely sound but felt like memories inscribed in his very cells. They identified themselves as custodians—guardians of consciousness—that observed the unfolding of Earth's destiny. These beings explained that humanity was on the cusp of a decisive shift—a threshold where consciousness itself would expand or contract, perpetually oscillating between states of potential and collapse. As Ahmed listened, the boundaries of self dissolved; his mind intertwined with theirs, entering a space where the very fabric of time and space became fluid, malleable, almost alive with possibility.

He perceived Earth not as a fixed point in space but as a complex web of probability streams—futures shimmering like mirages, some luminous and life-affirming, others darkened by unawareness and despair. In this realm of pure awareness, Lawrence's pursuit was revealed as initiation—an esoteric pilgrimage into the heart of existence, guided by a deeper understanding that to be human was to be a nexus, a node where infinite potential gathered. As these ideas unfurled within him, the revelation became a heavy, beautiful burden: the universe was a liquid ocean of possibility, and consciousness was the vessel shaping its depths. Higher beings watched over this unfolding dance, quietly orchestrating the emergence of new life—new reality—on a grand, incomprehensible scale. In that moment, Ahmed understood that Lawrence's legacy was more than a myth; it was a map—a call to those who dared to realize that heroism was rooted not in dominance but in the awakening of the shadow and light within.

As dawn approached, the entities withdrew, leaving Ahmed alone beneath the shattered sky. Yet, he was no longer the same. His awareness had stretched beyond reason, his senses attuned to a harmony that vibrated across space and time. In the quiet of the ruins, he found Lawrence's journals, now illuminated by an inner glow, revealing a final, unspoken message in Lawrence's own handwriting: "Find Sahra Al-Zaman." For the first time, Ahmed recognized the true strength of the heroes—those who venture into the shadowed depths of consciousness to reclaim light, not just for themselves but for the collective. His hands trembled as he clutched the fragile, crystalline relic left behind—a fragment of a reality far richer and more intricate than any contained within old manuscripts or academic theories. It was an invitation, a challenge, and a promise intertwined, beckoning him onward into the infinite, where shadows and heroes dance in eternal spectrum of human potential.

***

Eleven

The Threshold Revealed

Dr. Ridha's Dimensional Passage

In the hushed waning light of dusk, the Dorset heathland stretched out like a vast, breathing organism—its silent contours etched with shadows, whispering secrets of ages long past. The wind carried a faint, tremulous hum, perhaps the echoes of ancient voices or the restless stirring of forces unnamed. Dr. Ahmed Ridha sat motionless behind the wheel of his battered car, the engine winking out like a dying ember, leaving him immersed in a hush deeper than silence itself. Every fiber in his body braced for dissonance, yet beneath it all, an inexplicable pull tugged him toward the jagged horizon, as if the land itself beckoned him into the unknown.

Heightened senses prickling, Ahmed stepped out into the cool evening air, his boots crunching softly upon the gravel. The landscape before him was a shifting mosaic, a canvas of gnarled birch and rhododendron, where shadows grew heavy and the fading light seemed reluctant to surrender. Somewhere nearby, the legendary Clouds Hill loomed, yet what he encountered was no longer that familiar relic of Lawrence's refuge but an irregular outcrop of stone and weathered wood—its architecture a tangled web of Arts and Crafts motifs and unfamiliar, almost ancestral designs. The air was thick with the scent of damp earth and something more subtle—an essence that hinted at timelines overlapping, realities dimly bleeding into one another. The moment he crossed the threshold, the very fabric of space seemed to writhe and bend around him.

Inside, the cottage's interior defied every expectation. First, there was the disarming mixture of relics and manuscripts—editions of Burton's Arabian Nights sharing space with Doughty's Arabia Deserta, Persian miniatures swirling with intricate detail, and Bedouin silver glinting beneath dim lantern light. The walls appeared to pulse with stories, stories that vibrated with unseen energy, as if history had pressed itself into every crack and crevice. At the heart of this sanctuary sat Lady Edith Carrington, her posture unyielding, her gaze lantern-bright with a knowing that stretched beyond mere age or experience. Without preamble, she poured a cup of rare pu-erh tea, steam rising like a whisper of vaporized memory, and offered it to Ahmed as if their meeting was predestined—a fragment of time she kept carefully preserved.

As they sipped, Edith's voice weaved through the dim light, describing Lawrence's gatherings that seemed more myth than memory—an intimate coterie gathered before the fire, where Lawrence recited passages from the Quran in flawless Arabic, his voice a deep, lyrical pulse that held the room in suspended attention. Sassoon, scribbling furiously, captured the rhythms with feverish enthusiasm, while Augustus John sketched Lawrence's restless gestures, framing them forever on parchment. Edith's voice softened, yet her words sharpened, revealing that Lawrence's retreat into Clouds Hill was no mere act of escapism but a deliberate foray into the deeper currents of time itself. She claimed—her tone intimate, almost conspiratorial—that Lawrence had discovered anomalies in the land, phenomena rooted in the very essence of Dorset's ancient soil, phenomena that defied conventional science and challenged the established boundaries of reality.

With a slow, deliberate gesture, Edith retrieved a leather-bound volume—Lawrence's personal journals, purportedly lost in the chaos of 1919, their pages now laid bare before Ahmed. The handwriting was unmistakable—sharp, flowing script that carried the weight of unspoken truths. The entries spoke of "chronal disruptions," disturbances in the fabric of reality experienced during his campaigns, where time seemed to fold and unravel. Detailed sketches of craft beyond known technology flickered across the pages, cryptic diagrams illustrating constructs that appeared both mechanical and divine. These weren't the scribblings of a military strategist alone but of a scientist-half mystic, exploring the boundary where consciousness and the universe intertwined, blurring the line between fiction and fact in ways that dared to suggest the impossible.

Then Edith's voice grew even softer, revealing that Lawrence's elusive dedication "To S.A." in Seven Pillars of Wisdom did not symbolize a mere personal tribute. It concealed a secret—an abbreviation for "Sahra Al-Zaman," the Desert of Time—a metaphysical realm Lawrence had envisioned as an intersection point of cosmic currents. For Lawrence, the desert was no longer just arid land but a nexus of power and consciousness, a gateway through which the soul could traverse dimensions unseen. Edith claimed that Lawrence had learned to perceive these portals, that his retreat was a reconnaissance into the mutable nature of time itself—an exploration of the fabric that underpins reality, hidden in plain sight beneath the shifting sands of history.

Night deepened, and the darkness became alive. Edith's tales shimmered with an otherworldly glow, a chorus of whispers from realms beyond human perception. She described herself as a guardian—one of many—standing watch over these hidden intersections, channels that connected Earth to a vast tapestry of consciousness across space and time. Her stories painted Lawrence as more than a soldier or explorer; he was a seeker who glimpsed the infinite, his work a sacred mission to monitor and preserve the delicate balance of these unseen currents. Under the canopy of stars, Ahmed felt the fabric of his logical worldview fray, dissolving at its edges like morning mist retreating before the dawn.

The pivotal moment arrived precisely at 3:17 a.m., a time Edith called "Lawrence's hour," when the universe seemed to ripple and shimmer in response to an unseen harmonic. Out in the darkness, the sky fractured—an ancient parchment tearing apart to reveal a phantasmagoric tableau. Above Clouds Hill, a craft emerged—fluid, shimmering, incomprehensible—hovering like a question mark suspended in the fabric of reality. Its surface was in perpetual flux, shifting through states of polished metal, liquid light, and shimmering veils of ether that defied visual description. The craft's presence was an invitation—a summons that resonated deep within Ahmed's bones, tugging at the core of his consciousness with a gentle yet insistent pressure.

From the craft's interior, beings materialized—tall, luminous figures whose forms rippled between human and divine, their eyes portals into infinite worlds. Their consciousness flooded Ahmed, bypassing language altogether, communicating directly through shared thoughts—multilingual, layered, eternal. They explained that they were custodians—guardians of the evolution of consciousness—a collective of entities maintaining the delicate dance of awareness across the cosmos.

Their purpose was to observe the intersection points, those rare locations where human potential could transcend the ordinary, where future and past converged into a singular, luminous moment. Earth teetered now on the brink of a precipice, and these beings—these watchers—guided the brave and the curious toward a destiny unshackled by linear time.

In that moment—immense, silent, overwhelming—Ahmed's perception expanded beyond the limits of flesh and bone. He journeyed inward, beyond space, floating in a sea of pure consciousness, where the boundaries of identity dissolved. Colors pulsed with the heartbeat of the universe, sensations cascading like chords in a symphony of existence. The beings' messages echoed within him: Earth's evolution depended on the awakening of its inhabitants, on recognizing that time was not a river but an ocean of infinite currents accessible through heightened awareness and attunement. Their civilization existed in a state of perpetual becoming—an ongoing process of spiraling consciousness—beyond what human minds could grasp in ordinary waking life.

When Ahmed finally blinked back into his corporeal form, the night was a quiet void. The craft had vanished, leaving behind an air of quiet acknowledgment that passed through the landscape. The ruins of the cottage appeared unchanged but imbued with a profound significance—walls lined with Lawrence's long-lost correspondence, sketches, and maps marking the global nodes of these temporal currents. Among these relics, a battered typewriter stood silent and still, except for a single sheet of paper inscribed with Lawrence's final, flowing Arabic script: "Find Sahra Al-Zaman." The message was a key—an instruction wrapped in mystery and promise, urging Ahmed to step beyond all known borders into the liminal spaces of eternity.

His eyes fell upon the motorcycle—Lawrence's prized Brough Superior, gleaming as if freshly polished, an anachronism in the dawn's light. It beckoned him, not as a symbol of past deeds but as a vessel across the unseen currents he had glimpsed tonight. The sight of it sent a shiver through him—a silent vow that his journey was only beginning. As he approached, Ahmed sensed a presence—an unseen guide watching over, silently urging him toward the next phase of a destiny that had always been intertwined with the desert, the land, and the infinite layers of time itself. With careful hands, he grasped the device left behind—an unknown artifact pulsing with a subtle energy—and understood that he had been chosen to continue the work Lawrence had begun, not merely as a scholar but as a bridge into realms beyond consciousness.

The rising sun cast golden beams over the heath, illuminating the debris of the cottage and the quiet, enigmatic figure that now stood before it. Ahmed's heart hammered with a mixture of awe and purpose. His mind awoke to the truth that history and myth had been intertwined all along—that Lawrence's true quest extended far beyond military campaigns into the shifting currents of the soul, unseen by most yet accessible to those who dared to listen. The landscape around him shimmered faintly, revealing, for a moment, the shimmering veils of multiple probable futures—some luminous, others dark, all awaiting their moment to unfold. With resolve firming like steel in his veins, Ahmed turned his gaze outward, knowing that the journey beyond space and time had only begun, and that the threshold—once hidden—was now forever open.

***

The moment Ahmed stepped beyond the threshold, an unprecedented cascade of sensations engulfed him. It was as though the universe had unfurled a secret symphony, each note resonating through layers of consciousness he had never before perceived. Colors dissolved into sonic frequencies; hues he could not name vibrated with emotions he felt in his bones. What had once seemed contained within the boundaries of sight and sound now spiraled outward, dissonant and harmonious simultaneously, challenging every schema his mind had relied upon. The landscape itself began to pulse, shifting from tangible terrain to an energetic fabric woven from a thousand unseen threads.

His senses, suddenly unshackled from the usual constraints, sensed the unspoken beneath the spoken, the hidden beneath the visible. The air was thick with whispers—at times inaudible beneath a luminous hum, at others clear as the chime of a distant bell—telling stories that defied linguistic grasp. Every inhalation brought forth a bouquet of metaphysical scents: the scent of eternity, the tang of fleeting moments, the aroma of forgotten memories cloaked in the scent of the earth itself. Ahmed's skin prickled as textures unfurled—each grain of dirt and whisper of wind becoming a note in this vast sensory orchestra. It was relentless, pushing past boundaries, forcing him to confront the universe not as a collection of separate entities but as a interconnected, vibrating whole.

The landscape morphed with each passing moment. The hills of Dorset, familiar from countless childhood memories, shimmered into something more profound—a living construct of layered time and space. Ancient stones, moss-covered with centuries of silence, pulsed softly with a hidden energy—cosmic nodes whispering secrets through their silent presence. The chrome sheen of a distant craft flickered, flickering between dimensions, flickering in and out of visible reality. Winds carried fragments of memories from other dimensions, bringing with them faint echoes of voices long past—Sassoon's contemplative whispers, Lawrence's fierce debates, Edith's calm and knowing tone—all coalescing into an overwhelming auditory collage that defied cognition. His senses threatened to fracture under the weight of the multitudinous symphony, each element vying for his attention, each holding a fragment of the ultimate truth."

Then, as if in response to his inner chaos, a wave of pure light washed over him—a wave too expansive for the eye to contain. It poured from the fractured sky, spilling through the cracks in the fabric of space itself, illuminating sights and sounds beyond human understanding. Colors unraveled into melodies that resonated deep within, awakening chambers of his mind that had long been dormant. The ground beneath his feet thrummed with recognition—like a vast, ancient drum echoing the heartbeat of a universe in perpetual motion. This was no mere sensory overload; it was an awakening of consciousness, a symphony orchestrated by forces both beyond and within, merging the physical and spiritual in a crescendo that called into question the very nature of perception itself.

The cacophony reached its zenith as incomprehensible visuals appeared—phantasmagoric displays of geometric patterns, fractals spiraling into eternity, portals opening and closing in a dance of infinite possibility. Entwined in this grand procession were beings—luminous shapes that shimmered with intelligence, their forms shifting between human visage and abstract abstraction. Their presence felt almost like a song—notes flowing directly into his mind, bypassing all thought, injecting spatial memories and cosmic truths. Ahmed's perception curved, stretching into dimensions where time dissolved into a fluid continuum. Each moment stretched into eternity; each eternity condensed into a single instant of cosmic awareness. The sensation was chaos and harmony intertwined in an endless loop, demanding his surrender but also offering him a glimpse of the inherent unity underlying all apparent dissonance.

He felt himself dissolving, yet simultaneously becoming more himself than ever before—an observer unbound by linear constraints, immersed in a boundless field of consciousness. Images of worlds layered upon worlds flickered before him—futures where humanity rose into celestial awareness, and others dark with the specter of self-destruction, a stark reminder of his own responsibility. The multiplicity of worlds and realities pressed against his mind like a symphony reaching its climax, compelling him to see beyond the illusions of space and time. The being-like entities, now revealed as guardians of cosmic knowledge, communicated through waves of consciousness—each thought coding a universal truth: that human perception was but a shadow play behind a vast cosmic curtain, and that some individuals had the innate capacity to pierce its veils.

Within that maelstrom of sensation, Ahmed experienced a profound realization: the universe responded to awareness, bending and weaving itself around the intentions and states of consciousness. Time was not an arrow but a liquid ocean, its currents carrying souls and ideas through an infinite cascade of possibilities. The ancestors, mystics, and explorers that had paved the way whispered assurances in his mind —a silent chorus affirming that humanity's awakening was imminent, that the threshold was approaching. As the waves of perception receded, leaving him trembling but enlightened, he understood that this overload was not chaos but a divine symphony—an invitation to participate in the ongoing act of creation. To him, it was now clear: the universe's deepest melodies lay just beyond perceptual reach, waiting for those brave enough to listen beyond the noise into the silence beneath.

***

The night had settled heavily over Dorset's rugged heathland, a darkness so profound it seemed to swallow the horizon itself, leaving only the glow of distant stars to punctuate the void. As Ahmed drove, the rhythmic hum of his engine faltered, spluttering into silence amid the whispering trees, their skeletal forms reaching like silent sentinels into the indigo sky. The landscape, normally viewed as mundane, now appeared distorted—shadows flickered in unnatural contortions, and the wind carried an almost imperceptible vibration, as if the earth itself were restless beneath his wheels. Disoriented, he stepped out into the chilling silence, feeling an inexplicable pulse that resonated beneath his feet, a subtle reminder that this place, this moment, was not merely another journey's end but a threshold of something far greater.

The fog thickened, coalescing into shimmering wisps that seemed to form patterns—glyphs, perhaps, or memories etched into the fabric of the land's consciousness. Ahmed's eyes caught a flicker of movement—a fleeting silhouette near the ruins of Clouds Hill, a shape that defied conventional understanding. His breath caught as the outline of a figure materialized, standing as if summoned from the void, an entity of luminous translucence that seemed to hum with the very sinews of space and time. In this moment, reality wavered; the rational was dissolving into the realm of the ineffable. It was as if the landscape itself had become a living record, holding secrets that beckoned him to listen beyond the limits of his senses, nudging him closer to a truth hidden within the very core of existence.

From the shadows, a voice—soft yet resonant—emanated, weaving through the silent language of thought and sound. "You seek understanding," it whispered, "but what you seek is not confined to the confines of your mind or your history." The entity's form shimmered, rippling like a mirage, revealing glimpses of a civilization that had long transcended form, a collective consciousness pulsing with light and unbounded purpose. Ahmed felt an unbidden compulsion to surrender rationality—to let his perceptions expand and accept that he stood at a nexus where human history, cosmic forces, and conscious evolution intertwined. As images flooded his mind—visions of ancient worlds, quantum currents, and the endless dance of energies—he realized this was no longer a mere philosophical question, but a call to participate in a process of collective ascent far beyond what he'd ever imagined possible.

The beings from beyond the linear timeline moved with a grace that defied physical description, their forms shimmering between solidity and fluidity. As they approached, their thoughts communicated directly—an intricate web of understanding—delivering revelations that shimmered like fractured light across the corridors of Ahmed's consciousness. They spoke of "nexus points"—locations on earth where time's fabric had been woven with threads of consciousness so delicate yet so potent that even a subtle shift could ripple through the fabric of reality. These places, they explained, were gateways—foci of potential where evolution could leap forward or spiral into chaos, depending on human awareness. Humanity, in its ignorance, had until now trampled blindly across this tapestry, unaware that each step was edging closer to a junction—an intersection of possibility and destiny—whose significance transcended mere linear history.

Within this panoramic view, the cosmic custodians detailed the profound truth: Earth was not merely a planet spinning in space, but a living node in an infinitesimal network of consciousness extending through unfathomable layers of existence. Time was no longer a river flowing inevitably from past to future but a liquid ocean—its currents twisting, rippling, and shimmering with multiple potentialities. With each ripple, worlds branched beyond the immediate comprehendible—futures where humanity had awakened to its divine origins, and others where it had succumbed to fear and hubris, becoming dust upon the cosmic trail. It became clear that Lawrence's astonishing endeavors, his obsession with the desert's silence and the retreat into the intangible, had been an effort to grasp these currents—to tune into the frequencies of the universe itself. Was his retreat merely a withdrawal, or a deliberate step into the vortex of unfolding consciousness?

As the luminous entities continued their transmission, Ahmed's senses intensified—colors unseen by human eyes flooded his inner vision, sounds beyond sound vibrated in his skull, and he perceived a layered reality composed of countless possibilities simultaneously unfolding. These beings, as old as the universe itself, had transcended the limitations of form and time—beings who had long since merged into a state of becoming rather than being, a consciousness in perpetual expansion. They declared that Earth's imminent threshold was a point of no return, where the human soul—if awakened—could navigate across dimensions and attain an awareness that surpasses even the greatest of myths and legends. It dawned on Ahmed that his own journey was intertwined with this vast, silent evolution—a quest to discover where he truly belonged in this cosmic web—not as a detached observer, but as an active participant in a process that could either elevate or annihilate the consciousness of his kind.

Their words lingered like echoes of distant thunder, resonating within him with an undeniable sense of urgency. Before he could respond, a sudden shift—an influx of energy—thrust him into a state where space and time blurred into a kaleidoscopic dance. He felt himself dissolving into a formless existence—an influx of pure awareness—where he saw the intricate interplay of probabilities, the delicate balance of futures that hung trembling on the edge of realization. In this space, he glimpsed civilizations flourishing or failing; planets awakening to higher states of being or spiraling back into darkness. All of it, he understood, hinged on moments of recognition—signs buried within the fabric of reality, waiting for awakening minds to light their paths.

When finally he regained his senses, the cathedral silence returned, and the luminous entities faded into the ether, leaving behind only the echo of their presence. Ahmed found himself standing amidst debris—a ruin of what once might have been a humble cottage, yet now bore the mark of something far greater. As dawn's first light seeped into the remnants, he noticed that beneath layers of dust and decay, hidden walls revealed themselves—a secret archive of written words, sketches, and artifacts that Goethe would have called "signatures of eternity." Among these relics, the weathered pages of Lawrence's journals lay open, their ink dark and urgent. One passage caught his eye—a phrase scrawled in hurried Arabic script—"Sahra Al-Zaman," the Desert of Time, hinting at a place or a state of being where the fabric of reality itself could be surveyed, manipulated, or transcended.

He reached for the journals, feeling the weight of history and the whispers of unspoken knowledge. The pages seemed alive, whispering secrets in a language older than words; each line a portal, each diagram a story of consciousness unbound. As he untethered himself from the familiar, his attention was drawn to a small, crystalline object nestled among the debris—a fragment of some ancient technology, shimmering with iridescence, its surface humming softly as if charged with a subtle, luminous force. As he stared, the landscape around him dissolved into a montage of visions—maps marking nexus points, faces of companions who had descended into mystical realms, and glimpses of human destiny intertwined with cosmic currents. And in that fleeting moment, Ahmed understood his mission: to walk the path of Lawrence, to find the "Desert of Time," and to serve as a bridge—an authorized seeker—between the epoch of forgetfulness and the awakening that could reshape human history itself.

***

Twelve

Earth's Multiple Probabilities

Futures Unfolding

The landscape stretched out before him like a vast, breathing canvas; the wind whispered secrets through the gnarled branches of the ancient oaks, their silhouettes etched against a sky bleeding into dusk. Ahmed's hands clenched the steering wheel with a tremor he couldn't quite suppress, the car's engine suddenly faltering,Death's quiet hand stalling his journey in mid-flight. The broken machinery seemed like a silent gatekeeper, refusing passage, as if the very Earth conspired to draw him into her secret depths. Shadows lengthened, stretching across the heathland, beckoning him toward an unknown darkness that shimmered with the promise of revelation.

In that moment of stillness, the boundary between the physical and the unseen blurred. The fractured glass of his windshield reflected fractals of the darkening sky, rippling like consciousness itself—fluid, elusive, and whispering of dimensions beyond ordinary perception. Every nerve in his body tingled with anticipation and dread, the kind that comes when the mind is on the cusp of embracing truths it has long resisted. His rational worldview, forged through years of scholarly rigor, began to dissolve like sugar melting in hot water, its boundaries melting into infinite possibility. Here, on the edge of what he knew and what he could not yet comprehend, the universe seemed to pulse with a life of its own, waiting to unveil its secret faces.

Lights flickered from within the rambling bungalow nestled among the thickening foliage—half-hidden by rhododendrons, their waxy leaves glistening like silent sentinels guarding the threshold. The structure's architecture, stark yet inviting, bore the quiet authority of a place built long before the modern world had shaped it. As Ahmed hesitated, a figure emerged from the shadows—a woman whose bearing bespoke aristocratic endurance preserved through epochs. Her presence commanded the space, a timeless grace resting on her shoulders with the weight of countless histories. She approached with measured steps, her eyes luminous yet calm, revealing both worlds she had traversed and those she now welcomed him into. Her voice, when she spoke, was soft yet steadfast, wrapping around him like a shawl woven from threads of unspoken knowledge.

Inside, the air thrummed with an astonishing richness—shelves bowed beneath the weight of first editions and manuscripts. Persian miniatures, rendered with meticulous care, clung to the walls, their colors deepening in the subdued light. Bedouin silver, tarnished yet glowing with a hidden fire, adorned each surface as if guarding the whispers of centuries. Flipping through a leather-bound journal, Lady Edith Carrington paused to pour the pungent aroma of a rare pu-erh—her hands revealing the delicate touch of a seasoned custodian of secrets. She recounted stories of Lawrence that felt less like tales and more like readings from the fabric of eternity itself. The flickering fire cast shadows that danced and shifted, echoing her words about Lawrence reciting Quranic passages with fervor in the cold of night, his voice resonating like a prayer stitched into the very air, while Sassoon sketched and Augustus John thrashed about in restless sketches of a man haunted by visions not just of war, but of unseen worlds intertwined with their own.

But then, slowly, her narrative unraveled the familiar, revealing layers previously hidden behind historical veneer. She described Lawrence's retreat to Clouds Hill not as retreat at all, but as an active probing of dimensions beyond the linear—an exploration of temporal anomalies that made the Dorset countryside itself a living mirror of the infinite. Lady Edith, her eyes dark with shared secrets, claimed that her own childhood memories had been shaped by encounters with these phenomena—occasions when time seemed to shift, when moments stretched and folded like the fabric of a cosmos aware of its own reflection. Her words became more insistent, a subtle call to trust her as she produced Lawrence's journals—journals that supposedly vanished in the chaos of the Suez Canal incident, yet now lay open before him, their pages filled with handwriting unmistakably Lawrence's, brimming with observations about "chronological displacements" and "temporal currents" that ended in sketches of bizarre craft, machines unlike any known technology, shimmering with impossible geometries. It was as if the very pages pulsed with a dormant energy, whispering that earth had been stitched with pathways only the initiated could glimpse.

Ahmed's skepticism wavered, his intellect straining to grasp the implications, yet still clutching at the safe notions of cause and effect. Edith's words beckoned him deeper—beyond the confines of logic—into a metaphysical labyrinth where time was malleable, akin to a liquid that could be stirred and shaped by consciousness. Her revelation—the true meaning of Lawrence's dedication "To S.A."—transformed from a cryptic reference into a portal of understanding: "Sahra Al-Zaman"—the Desert of Time—was a state of consciousness, a realm where the desert's emptiness concealed nodes of immense power, intersections of multiple currents woven into the earth itself. She claimed that Lawrence's obsession was not conquest, but attunement—to these nodes, to potentialities, to the malleability of reality itself. The vast empty sands of Arabia mirrored these points, his experiences an early warning sign for those who could sense the invisible strings suspending the universe, waiting for a conscious awakening to pull them into harmony.

Night deepened, shrouding the landscape in a silken cloak that seemed to hum with the vibrations of other dimensions. Lady Edith's voice softened, yet retained an electric charge. She admitted her role was that of a guardian, a silent overseer of the earth's temporal gateways—places where beings from beyond linear time watched and waited, bound in a dance of eternal vigilance. The entities, she explained, were luminous, formless, and evolving—higher consciousnesses that communicated telepathically, their thoughts threading seamlessly into the minds of those prepared to receive. They were custodians of the threshold, watching over humanity's journey toward a collective transcendence, knowing that the moment had approached when humans would stand on the brink of a leap into cosmic awareness. The air crackled with anticipation, as if even the atmosphere itself bowed under the weight of destined transformation.

The climax approached when, at precisely 3:17 AM—what Edith called "Lawrence's hour"—a resonant harmony stirred in the darkness. Outside, the sky tore apart like ancient parchment, revealing a vortex of shimmering light that defied ordinary perception. The craft appeared—an impossible sculpture of fluid metal and shimmering liquid light, shifting between form and formlessness in a dance older than human history. As it hovered, entities—luminous beings of incomprehensible grace—descended, their presence transcending biological limitations, their consciousness apparent in waves of thought. They spoke directly into Ahmed's mind—Arabic, English, and echoes of primordial languages—revealing that the universe was alive with consciousness, that Earth itself was a nexus of potentialities, waiting for those who could navigate its currents. The beings depicted a civilization that existed outside time, eternally becoming, examining Earth's role as a crucible of evolution. To them, humanity's future depended on awakening to this deeper truth, recognizing its own divine origin within the cosmic fabric.

Ahmed's senses expanded into a kaleidoscope of sights, sounds, and sensations. Dimensions opened around him as he felt himself dissolving into a sea of consciousness—no longer a confined entity but a wave riding the currents of infinite possibility. He saw worlds branching, futures and pasts coalescing into streams of potential, and realized that the guardians' message was clear: Earth's fate was written in the choices made now, in full awareness or endless ignorance. He understood that the core of all existence was the creative power of thought—energy shaping reality, perception molding time—and that the heroes, mystics, and even conflicts of history were merely reflections of this primal force. Rising from this communion, Ahmed awakened again on the dew-damped heath, yet something fundamental had shifted within him, as if he carried a seed of understanding that would blossom only when the moment arrived. As dawn breached the horizon, he clutched a strange crystalline fragment, a fragment that vibrated with the echoes of some ancient song, whispering that the gateway—the true nexus—was within reach. The haunting yet exhilarating realization settled: human consciousness was poised to leap beyond its limitations, into a realm of infinite becoming. The universe, in its silent, infinite song, was waiting for us to listen and answer.

***

Ahmed's eyes fluttered open to the fractured glow of dawn seeping beneath the cracked edges of the cottage's veranda. A faint hum vibrated in the air, not heard with ears but felt—a rhythmic pulse that resonated deep within his bones, reverberating through the fabric of what he once believed to be reality. The remnants of the night's vision lingered—as if a dream still clung to his consciousness—yet his surroundings insisted on their mundane solidity, the broken furniture and dust-laden shelves a stark contrast to the celestial symphony that had recently unfolded. He sat upright slowly, his pulse uneven, questioning whether he had crossed some invisible boundary or merely conjured a spectral echo of his own imagination. An ancient, almost imperceptible trembling coursed through him, hinting at truths lying just beyond the veil of the known.

Outside, the landscape was draped in a soft, pallid light; the heathland stretched in undulating waves of heather and bracken, whispering secrets carried on a breeze that felt more like a caress from another realm than ordinary wind. The air was thick with a scent of ogham stones and distant fires, as if the land itself remembered how to speak in a language older than time. Ahmed moved toward the shattered window, the glass crackling under his fingers as fragments shifted within their frames, revealing a sky fractured like gossamer silk torn by unseen forces. Above him, the sky wavered—a mosaic of shifting colors, strange constellations swirling in a pattern that defied conventional astronomy, opening a portal to something far beyond the limits of his understanding. His heart hammered with the unnameable sense that he had stepped into a space where every rule of physics and history unraveled, revealing depths where consciousness itself was fluid and mutable.

Then, a presence—calm, luminous, and immense—descended into his awareness without words, a consciousness shimmering just beyond opacity. It moved through his mind as a breeze moves through leaves—coalescing, dispersing, awakening dormant habitats within him. He felt his old knowledge flicker like a dying star, replaced by visions of events intertwined through a web of cosmic currents predicting futures and histories layered atop one another. These were not mere images but a complex dance of probabilities, each thread tugging at the fabric of his identity. The beings of light—tall, shimmering silhouettes—aligned around him like sentinels of the threshold, their presence whispering in a language of thought, their collective consciousness expanding and contracting as if they were breathing the universe itself. As their silent voice opened the doorway within his mind, Ahmed understood—this was no longer merely a vision. It was a call to navigate a realm where time was a liquid, flowing in endless ripples and currents, and each ripple carried the potential to reshape the course of history itself.

***

The evening air hung heavy, almost oppressive, as Ahmed stepped out of his battered car, the engine's stutter echoing strangely in the stillness. The landscape stretched before him like a ghostly tapestry—ancient heathland cloaked in shadow, whispers of wind threading through the gnarled branches. The fading light cast long, darkening silhouettes, each tree and curve of heather seeming to conceal secrets that had whispered for centuries. A sensation of being watched prickled across his skin, but he shook it off—yet a trace of unease persisted, like the faint static of an unseen signal vibrating just beyond comprehension.

As he moved closer to the place where the road had failed him, an uncanny stillness seemed to settle over the land. The familiar contours of Bovington Heath now appeared liminal, as if caught between worlds, inviting him into a space just beyond ordinary perception. His mind jittered between skepticism and curiosity, the rational anchor buried deep within him struggling to hold sway. Then, from the darkness emerged a faint, golden glow—a preternatural illumination spilling from the shadows, beckoning him forward into the unknown. Each step felt weighted, as if the ground beneath him resonated with a deeper, dormant energy, awakening as night fell fuller around him.

Just beyond the fringe of the heath, he discovered something altogether unexpected: a rambling structure cloaked amidst the greening rhododendrons and silvery birch trees, its architecture delicate yet oddly timeless. The building's exterior, fashioned in Arts and Crafts style, suggested a predating of Lawrence's famous retreat—a place that carried whispers of stories long before the well-worn legends of Clouds Hill. Warm light streamed from its windows, and on the veranda sit a figure emitting an aura of aristocratic grace—an elderly woman whose bearing seemed carved from history itself. She turned smoothly at the sound of his footsteps, her eyes—bright yet inscrutable—welcoming yet guarded, as if holding secrets too precious for casual revelation.

"You've come far," she said softly, her voice like a gentle ripple in still water, "and perhaps you seek answers only the night can give."

The interior defied all expectations attached to its modest front; walls lined with bound volumes and delicate Persian miniatures created an atmosphere thick with memory and meaning. First editions of Burton's Arabian Nights shared shelf space with Doughty's Arabia Deserta, hinting that this sanctuary was a nexus of stories and histories that blurred the lines between myth and reality. Silver and lapis lazuli adornments shimmered amid the shadows, each artifact seemingly radiating its own silent chronicle. Lady Edith Carrington, as she introduced herself, moved with the practiced ease of someone intimately acquainted with time's hidden corridors, pouring tea so fragrant that a scholar's rational defenses wavered in its wake. As she handed him the delicate porcelain cup, her gaze lingered on his, a conspiratorial smile hinting at truths far beyond the superficial realm of academia.

Ahmed's doubts simmered beneath her impassive exterior, but her subsequent stories—a series of vignettes—began to unravel his skepticism. She recalled nights of Lawrence pacing before a fireplace, reciting passages from the Quran with perfect cadence, while Sassoon scribbled notes and Augustus John sketched restless figures in the dim light. She detailed unfiltered debates with Nancy Astor over the future shape of the Arab world, battles of intellect that stretched long into the night, and moments when Lawrence's restless energy seemed more than human—for he was, she claimed, probing realms that defied simple understanding. But what imprisoned his true purpose was her assertion that his retreat to Clouds Hill was no mere refuge from war, but a deliberate crossing point—a physical manifestation of a deeper, more enigmatic pilgrimage into the anatomy of time itself. Her words hung in the air, heavy with implication: Lawrence was investigating phenomena that challenged the linear fabric of history, occurrences that he believed could be harnessed or even controlled.

Then, unexpectedly, Edith reached for a leather-bound journal—Lawrence's own, preserved through some miraculous channel—and handed it to Ahmed with reverence. The pages, though aged, were undeniably authentic, their ink dark and flowing, filled with scientific-style notes on "chronological displacement," observations of "time anomalies," and sketches of craft unlike any known aircraft—objects that seemed to shimmer with the spectral energy of other realities. Her voice softened as she revealed that Lawrence's famous dedication in Seven Pillars of Wisdom—"To S.A."—wasn't a mere initial, but a cryptic acknowledgment of "Sahra Al-Zaman," a term evoking the mystical, metaphysical "Desert of Time." According to her, Lawrence had believed certain Earth locations vibrated at intersections of temporal currents, places where the long threads of history and future converged into a single point—an invisible crossroad that revealed the true malleability of time itself. Her words resonated deep within Ahmed's understanding, unsettling the foundation of the solid rationalism he thought defined his identity.

The night deepened despite their impassioned conversation. An almost imperceptible harmonic hum filled the room—a resonance that subtly vibrated through walls and consciousness alike, hinting at energies beyond the senses. Edith's tone shifted, her voice almost whispering, as she described her role as a guardian of this nexus—an eternal watcher tasked with safeguarding the delicate balance between worlds. She shared stories of beings from beyond what humans could see—entities made of pure awareness, "luminous and formless," who monitored civilizations from realms untouched by linear time. These beings, she claimed, communicated through thoughts, not words, their messages cascading directly into the mind like threads of light aimed at awakening dormant truths. The implication was inescapable: Earth was a hub of unseen currents, and humanity stood at a crossroads—choices that could decide whether the world would awaken to its divine potential or spiral into chaos. With each revelation, Ahmed felt his rationalist veneer crack further, the scientific veneer peeling back to expose the trembling core of something vast—and unfathomable.

Suddenly, Edith's words faded into a different timbre. "Tonight is 'Lawrence's hour'," she murmured, eyes gleaming with a mixture of reverence and anticipation. 3:17 AM—an exact moment she identified as vital—when Lawrence himself would often mount his motorcycle and race into the night's embrace, chasing a shadow-world only he sensed. From the shadows outside, a strange, harmonic resonance swelled—both felt and heard—an ebb and flow that seemed to beckon Ahmed beyond the physical boundaries of the room. Against his will, his feet moved, compelled by an unseen tide. Stepping outside, he was greeted by a sky fractured into shards of shimmering parchment, a celestial display that seemed torn between dimensions. The clouds split like ancient scrolls, revealing a craft—an object of impossible grace, shimmering between form and fluid light, shifting endlessly through states of matter. Its surface rippled, reflecting fragments of stars, liquid silver, and a brilliance that defied definition. It hovered silently, established in a realm where time's rules unravel, revealing its true purpose: a vessel not just of travel, but of consciousness—an invitation to explore the infinite.

Then, the being emerged—tall, luminous, their forms suggesting evolution beyond human limitations, shimmering with an inner radiance that spoke directly to the soul. Their presence pressed into Ahmed's mind, their thoughts decipherable in languages older than words—Arabic, English, and echoes of ancient dialects—melding into a symphony of intent. These custodians of awareness explained that Earth's future depended on recognizing the signals woven into the very fabric of reality—on understanding that consciousness, not matter, was the primal force of creation. They unveiled the idea that time was a liquid, flowing in currents, ripples, and eddies—accessible to those who could sense its subtlety. Lawrence, they stated, was a bridge—someone who learned to navigate these currents—a pioneer of higher awareness, charged with guiding humanity toward the threshold of cosmic consciousness. As they spoke, Ahmed's perception expanded—his sense of self dissolving into the vast ocean of possibility, the boundaries of space and time dissolving until only pure awareness remained, shimmering at the precipice of eternity.

When he awoke, the cold dawn greeted him in the ruins of the once-grand cottage—the debris, the fractured walls, the scattered artifacts—all seemed imbued with a hidden language. Among them, he discovered Lawrence's journal, its pages delicate but still resistive to decay, bearing the final, flowing script: "Find Sahra Al-Zaman." The message pulsated with purpose, an oracle for those who could hear it. Hidden beneath layers of dust and time, he uncovered Lawrence's artifacts—maps of Arabia marked in his hand, photographs showing figures enshrouded in light, and a peculiar collection of sketches—crafts not of this world. Their fluid shapes seemed to ripple with life, hinting at higher realms of existence. Near the ruins, he found Lawrence's motorcycle, polished and ready as if awaiting its next journey—a relic of a man who once dared to cross boundaries unknown. And in a concealed compartment of Edith's hidden archive, he discovered a recent entry, written long after Lawrence's death—a message in Edith's meticulous hand: "He's been chosen. The bridge between worlds now spans both past and future. And Ned's work remains unfinished."

As the sun crested the horizon, casting a golden hue over the heath, Ahmed gazed towards the sky, where a figure in leather and goggles tore across the fields—an image both familiar and uncanny, as if Lawrence himself refused to fade into obscurity. The figure's speed betrayed urgency, a pursuit beyond the realm of ordinary understanding, a race to catch what lingers just beyond perception. Ahmed's heart hammered with a mixture of awe and dread, the realization sinking that this was not merely a legend but an ongoing dialogue with higher dimensions. Turning back, he saw the cottage revert to its dilapidated state, yet he carried with him proof—an iridescent crystal, pulsing softly, embodying the very essence of what he had glimpsed. More than relic or relics, these objects held the key to a truth long hidden: Lawrence's true mission, a sacred knowledge of the desert as a portal—an unseen corridor that links consciousness across infinite time. Ahmed understood, then, that his destiny intertwines with these currents, that every step he takes now echoes within a universe where the choice to ascend or fall resides with each individual—a choice that will determine whether humanity survives its own forgetfulness or blossoms into cosmic awareness. The warning—the call to awareness—resounded through the silence, a summons to stand at the crossroad of worlds where the future waits, shimmering, just beyond the edge of sight.

***

Thirteen
The Responsibility of Awareness
Knowledge and Power

The dusk had settled like a heavy velvet drape over the Dorset heath, shadows lengthening and merging into one another as if the landscape itself was melting into a single, ancient consciousness. Ahmed's hands trembled slightly on the steering wheel, the engine's choked cough echoing the slow unraveling of his certainty. Discontented but strangely unperturbed by the mechanical failure, he stepped out into the chilly air, the scent of damp earth and bracken filling his senses. Around him, the heath stretched endlessly, whispering secrets in the wind—an echo of times when the land was a living, breathing archive of unseen currents. The stillness seemed almost palpable, pressing against his skin, hinting at the unspoken gateways lurking beneath the mundane fabric of reality, waiting for those brave enough to notice them.

The landscape's quieting gave way to a mounting sense of dislocation, a feeling that perhaps the very ground beneath his feet was more than mere earth; it was a nexus of invisible strings, woven across dimensions long hidden from human view. As he moved toward the faint glow emanating from the nearby ruin—an architecturally curious bungalow seemingly out of place amid the wild heath—an awareness flickered in the back of his mind, a whisper of a different truth. The bungalow's architecture, with its deliberate asymmetry and handcrafted details, seemed to hum with an unspoken purpose, as if built expressly to conceal secrets beyond the reach of linear time. The warm light beckoned him, a beacon in the twilight, and he hesitated only briefly before crossing the threshold into that strange portal of history and mystery.

Inside, the air shimmered with familiarity yet carried the charge of something utterly unfamiliar. Shelves lined with first editions of Burton, Doughty, and rare Persian miniatures formed a labyrinth that beckoned both the scholar and the seeker. Walls were adorned with maps of Arabia, annotated in a script that seemed to pulse with living memory, while artifacts—silver ornaments, sketches of aircraft that defied conventional understanding—dangled and leaned as if waiting for recognition. Lady

Edith Carrington, an embodiment of aristocratic calm, sat gracefully on a velvet armchair, her presence transforming the modest interior into a chamber of sacred relics. She poured tea with a precise, practiced gesture, offering Ahmed a cup that seemed to warm more than just his hands. Her voice, soft yet layered with the weight of centuries, initiated a dialogue that would challenge every notion of history and time he held dear.

As she began recounting her own history—her childhood witnessing phenomena that defied scientific explanation, her clandestine role as a guardian of unseen currents—Ahmed felt a slow unravelling within his rational mind. Her stories wove images of Lawrence, pacing before a fire, reciting verses in Arabic, Siegfried Sassoon scribbling furiously in a corner, and Edith herself standing at the edges of temporal disruptions whose upheavals felt woven into the fabric of her very existence. Her tales stretched beyond mere anecdotes; they hinted at a reality where time bent and shifted, where history's linear march was merely a surface layer concealing a dance of multidimensional currents. Each word she spoke was like a key unlocking another chamber of his understanding, yet simultaneously casting shadows of doubt that flickered with unsettling intensity.

The moment thickened as Edith produced Lawrence's journals, aged but remarkably intact. Their pages bore the unmistakable handwriting of a man obsessed not merely with military strategy, but with the nature of consciousness itself. Entries that read like scientific reports described displacement events, chronological anomalies, and sketches of strange craft—visions that resonated with the stories Edith had shared. Every sentence suggested Lawrence had explored realms where time warped and consciousness roamed freely beyond the confines of linear history. The air seemed to thicken with anticipation and the weight of forbidden knowledge, as though the pages themselves carried a dormant power, urging him to see beyond the illusion of cause and effect.

Edith's revelations culminated in the clarification of a cryptic dedication in *Seven Pillars of Wisdom*. It had long been assumed to honor a personal connection, perhaps a token of friendship or respect. Yet she insisted it was something far more profound: a homage to "Sahra Al-Zaman," the "Desert of Time"—a conceptual nexus point where reality's fabric was thinnest, revealing the malleability of existence. According to her, Lawrence had discovered that certain locations on Earth—intersections of unseen currents—could be accessed at moments of heightened awareness. To visit these was to step into a realm where past, present, and future intermingled in a chaotic, yet somehow harmonious dance. The desert, in this sense, was not merely a barren expanse, but a living, breathing nexus—an eternal doorway—whose power Lawrence sought to understand and harness.

Night deepened into an almost palpable entity, wrapping itself around the house and the surrounding heath, as Edith's voice took on a whispering timbre. She spoke of beings—higher entities—whose existence transcended physicality, guardians of the pathways that connect worlds and times. Here, at the edge of reality, Edith claimed to have witnessed interactions with these luminous presences, entities who communicated through thought rather than speech and monitored the evolution of consciousness across the cosmos. It was here, she said, that Lawrence's true mission had originated—not merely as an explorer of geopolitics, but as a voyager seeking the keys to higher states of awareness. Her words sounded like a secret hymn, stirring the very fabric of Ahmed's mind, dissolving the barriers built by years of empirical certainty.

And then, at precisely 3:17 in the morning—what Edith called "Lawrence's hour"—the air vibrated with an almost imperceptible hum, a resonance that resonated deep within his bones. Outside, the sky fractured like ancient parchment, revealing glimpses of impossible light. Before him floated a craft of divine complexity—its form endlessly shifting between polished metal, rippling liquid light, and a substance unnameable—an artifact of the higher dimensions, existing outside any known paradigm of physics. Tall, luminous beings materialized from the ether—whose presence seemed both a question and an answer—entities whose forms hinted of evolution beyond biological constraints. Their consciousness flooded into Ahmed's mind through a torrent of thoughts—insistent, serene, and incomprehensibly layered—speaking directly in languages that predated mankind's own speech. These beings explained their purpose: to serve as custodians of consciousness' evolution, guardians of the currents that bind our world to others, a role centuries in the making, now echoing toward him.

Their message was clear: Earth was approaching a monumental threshold, a pivotal point where humanity's collective awareness could surge into cosmic consciousness or fracture into chaos. The beings' civilization shimmered in a state of perpetual becoming, beyond the linear, swirling in a kaleidoscope of probabilities. Each potential future—either luminous or dark—reverberated through the cosmic fabric, a web of possibilities hinging on decision, recognition, awakening. As they explained, consciousness—illogically simple yet infinitely profound—was the active agent shaping the universe's unfolding. Time, they insisted, was a liquid, a vast ocean of possibility, and certain individuals—heroes, mystics, and those like Lawrence—were natural navigators within this great, flowing sea. Their role was to guide humanity toward the vantage point from which the currents of existence could be understood—and ultimately mastered.

The cosmic voyage didn't end there. Through the beings' silent guidance, Ahmed felt himself slipping into a realm of pure awareness—a place where space dissolved and only flickering impressions remained, hinting that the boundaries of self and universe were one and the same. The civilization he glimpsed was built entirely on the evolution of consciousness, echoing with unspoken truths of profound interconnectedness. From this vantage, Earth's myriad probability streams became visible—the light-filled future in which humankind transcended its limitations, and the shadowy one where ignorance and fear led to self-destruction. The choice was stark, yet crafted in subtlety—each step dependent on awakening, on recognizing the interconnected pattern that underpinned existence itself.

When Ahmed finally awoke, the primordial dawn seeped into a landscape forever altered in his mind. The ruins around him, though seemingly unchanged, had transformed into a vessel of profound memory—walls inscribed with the names of Lawrence, Sassoon, John, and Astor—testaments of a silent alliance across time. His fingertips traced the markings on the walls, grounding himself amidst the lingering echoes of the night's divine encounter. In the wardrobe, Lawrence's personal effects—uniform, maps, sketches—offered tangible links to a life that had traversed beyond known history into an unseen continuum. The motorcycle, gleaming as if recently ridden, seemed an artifact of a mystical journey, a marker of a man who had ventured into realms no ordinary soldier could comprehend.

Most startling was the discovery of a new inscription, delicately scrawled on a recovered sheet of Lawrence's journal: "Find Sahra Al-Zaman," it bid, invoking the ancient desert—a metaphysical space where time's fabric becomes unraveled. The message carried a weight of urgency, hinting that the key to the cosmic portal lay not in remote locations but within a consciousness accessible only to those daring enough to seek it. As the first light touched the horizon, Ahmed sensed that his role was no longer confined to academia or mere speculation. He was now intertwined with a living pattern—an imprint upon the fabric of reality itself—bound to carry the torch for humanity's next leap into the infinite. The physical world, once a barrier, was now a doorway—and the voyage into the unseen corridors of time and consciousness was just beginning.

***

As the midnight hour approached, the landscape around Bovington Heath seemed to hold its breath, the blackened sky fractured by a tremulous shimmer that defied earthly logic. Amidst the silent stretch of ancient oaks and whispering heather, luminous figures began to manifest, their forms shimmering with an ethereal light that pulsed in harmony with an unseen rhythm. Taller than humans, yet unbound by the dimensions of flesh and bone, they seemed to flicker between states of matter—sometimes solid, sometimes liquid, other times nothing more than a living illumination that danced like flames caught in perpetual motion. Their presence elicited a shiver that was not entirely fear but a profound recognition, as if awakening a buried memory from the depths of consciousness itself.

These beings, embodiments of pure awareness, hovered with serenity and purpose, existing beyond the constraints of physical form. Their luminous eyes held infinite wisdom—facets of centuries, millennia, perhaps eons—stitched together in a gaze that traversed worlds. Communication transcended language; thoughts flowed like a clear river, unburdened by words, impregnated with the gravity of knowledge that no human mind could readily grasp. A gentle hum, resonating like a sacred song, pervaded the air, vibrating within Ahmed's bones and awakening a silent dialogue situated in the corridors of mind and spirit. The beings regarded him not with curiosity or condescension, but with a quiet acknowledgment that he belonged to a destiny far greater than he had ever sensed, a role woven into the very fabric of cosmic unfolding.

The landscape, long considered just a relic of history and myth, shimmered under their gaze—each hill, each stone, each blade of grass pulsating with unseen currents of energy. They guided Ahmed's perception outward, revealing the ancient structure beneath the superficial earth—a labyrinth of divine architecture etched into the substratum of reality. Here, beneath the veneer of mundane existence, lay a grid of intersecting points that acted as gateways, gateways to multiple timelines, to uncharted states of consciousness. The guardians' existence hinged upon the delicate maintenance of these currents, their task to safeguard the pathways through which evolution progresses. To witness their work was to understand that Earth itself was a living, breathing nexus—an entity demanding respect and awareness from those who dared to seek its deeper truths.

Deepening the surreal meeting, Ahmed perceived that these entities weren't merely custodians of physical pathways but also navigators of consciousness—sentinels watching over the great transition looming ahead. Their awareness stretched into dimensions beyond time, their consciousness intertwined with the planet's own pulse. They communicated via vibrations that stirred the core of his being, guiding him toward understanding a universal truth: that awareness was the primal seed from which all creation emerged, flickering like a spark that could ignite infinite possibilities or burn away in destruction. Their presence was a reminder that human civilization, with all its hubris and forgetfulness, teetered on the brink of a revelation—one that required not only knowledge, but the active awakening of the mind's dormant powers. The guardians, eternal and unwavering, embodied that silent, relentless watchfulness, ensuring that the sacred currents remained intact amidst the cacophony of chaos.

Yet, amid this divine stillness, a sudden shift occurred—an intensification of that harmonic resonance, swelling into a crescendo that seemed to ripple through the very fabric of the universe. The sky above, fractured by the shimmering disturbance, split open wider, revealing glimpses of realms swirling in impossible geometries—domains where thought was action, where existence transcended the linear constraints of past, present, and future. In that dark, sacred space, Ahmed felt the boundaries of himself dissolving like fog at dawn. The guardians' luminous forms elongated, reaching out with tendrils of consciousness that beckoned him to step beyond the threshold of ordinary perception. An unspoken command pulsed through the air: to move, to accept, to see beyond the illusion of solidity, into the infinite potential of awareness as the true origin of all that is.

***

The dusk's dying light cast a subdued amber glow over Bovington Heath, shadows lengthening like dark tongues licking the edges of an awakening. With each mile driven, the landscape's silence deepened—an almost oppressive stillness that hinted at secrets etched deep within the earth's antiquated bones. Ahmed's thoughts felt suspended in a heavy aquamarine haze, the jarring whirr of the engine failing to match the weight of what lay ahead—an unconscious, stirring awareness gnawing at the borders of his rational mind. It was as if the landscape itself was whispering, urging him to pay heed to a message written into the very fabric of this barren, sprawling tapestry.

The fragile fabric of his assumptions, woven through years of scholarly discipline, was tearing. His research, once painstakingly dissected and measured, now shimmered with a new, unsettling clarity—an unvoiced call to recognize that beneath the surface of history, beneath the veneer of causality, there lurked a realm beyond comprehension. The rejection from his colleagues echoed like a distant storm, a reminder that mainstream academia remained tethered to familiar, linear histories—truths that dismissed the unseen currents coursing beneath the surface. Yet, within his core, an undeniable whisper persisted, insisting that the true narrative was far richer, layered with dimensions that refused to be confined by words or evidence alone.

As the terrain grew more rugged and the sky swelled with the approaching night, Ahmed's gaze drifted toward the sky—a vast canvas stitched with stars that shimmered with an unnatural, almost hypnotic radiance. Somewhere deep within, a sense of destiny flickered into life—a realization that his study of history was merely an outward reflection, a surface rippling on the immense cosmic waters. The landscape, with its silent witnesses—ancient oaks, stubborn stones, the ghostly presence of a forgotten time—began revealing its deeper purpose: as a threshold, a liminal space where worlds intersect, where time's fragile veneer thins to transparency.

Had he, like Lawrence, been summoned here by forces beyond his comprehension? Or was this destiny merely another illusion, a trap for the mind to unravel?

His heartbeat quickened as the car dared one more sputtering cough before surrendering entirely in a silent, final refusal. Turning off the engine, Ahmed stepped into the cool embrace of the evening, the air thickening with the scent of damp earth and moss. A sensation unfurled—a gentle but persistent urging within, as if unseen tendrils reaching into his consciousness, pulling him toward the shadowed outline of the landscape. Behind him, the broken machine lay silent, a symbol of limits shattered or perhaps only shifted. Ahead, the darkened silhouette of Clouds Hill loomed—a familiar monument to myth, but tonight, it felt strangely distant, like a doorway to an alternate realm.

As he moved toward the cottage, the boundary between certainty and doubt blurred. The ordinary had dissolved into a realm where meaning refused to be fixed, where the whispers of the wind carried voices of past voices—heroes, prophets, perhaps even spirits guarding the thin veil of reality. The patchwork of memory and myth seemed alive, pulsating with a rhythm that beckoned him further. When he finally reached the verandah, a figure was waiting—a figure whose presence was both genteel and impenetrably ancient, her bearing echoing aristocratic grandeur alongside a timeless serenity. Her eyes, glinting like polished obsidian, held the kind of calm that could either soothe or unsettle.

Lady Edith Carrington extended her hand with practiced grace, as if welcoming an old friend into a sacred space. Her voice, soft yet unmistakably deliberate, introduced her as someone who had long understood the language of the unseen—her words weaving through the air, hinting at truths that defied the mundane logic Ahmed held dear. Inside, the cottage's interior was a labyrinth of cultural memory: shelves bowed beneath the weight of first editions, Persian miniatures gazing silently from walls, and the faint scent of aged paper mingling with a spicy undertone of rare pu-erh tea. As she poured the dark, fragrant liquid, her gaze lingered—an opener of doors, a keeper of stories hidden within stories.

Her stories, delivered with a solemn intimacy, unraveled threads that challenged everything Ahmed thought he knew. Lawrence, she claimed, was more than a soldier or a diplomat—he was a seeker, a guardian of the thresholds between worlds. Tales of Lawrence reciting verses from the Quran in perfect Arabic around roaring fires, of Sassoon scribbling notes as Lawrence paced impatiently, and of great debates that stretched into dawn, painted a picture far removed from the distant, romanticized recollections. Edith's words suggested that Lawrence's retreat to Dorset was a deliberate act—an act of exploration into the fabric of time itself, an attempt to pierce the veils separating the known from the unnameable. And at the center of it all, an elusive nexus lay dormant, awaiting those who could recognize its signs.

The night's silence grew heavier, broken only by Edith's quiet revelations. She drew from the depths of her memory a name—one that made Ahmed's blood run cold: Sahra Al-Zaman—"The Desert of Time"—a concept that Lawrence had known, a realm where Earth's currents of consciousness intertwined and diverged. Her voice, filled with a reverence that bordered on worship, described how Lawrence had sensed these intersections, long before his exile into myth. The idea—that certain landscapes, like Dorset's barren moorlands, were not merely physical spaces but portals—became a seed, planting itself deep within Ahmed's consciousness. Suddenly, his academic skepticism faltered, trembling before the weight of this revelation—an invitation into a reality where time was not linear but fluid, where the past, present, and future danced in an eternal, restless waltz.

As the clock turned toward 3:17 AM—the moment Edith called "Lawrence's hour"—an almost imperceptible shift swept through the cottage's shadowed corners. The air thickened, palpable with an electric charge, and Ahmed found himself drawn outward, beyond the confines of his physical body. The sky fractured like an ancient, battered manuscript, revealing a shimmering craft of impossible beauty—its surface flickering between states of matter, shimmering with liquid light, shifting in ways that defied all logic or expectation. Tall, luminous beings emerged from this anomaly—forms of shimmering intelligence, a consciousness beyond human shape, their features suggestive of evolution unbound by biology. They communicated without words—thoughts flowing directly into Ahmed's mind, filling him with a vast, silent understanding.

The beings explained, in a harmony beyond language, that they were custodians of consciousness, explorers of the thresholds humanity had yet to fully understand. Their presence, they claimed, was to guide the evolution of awareness itself—an ascent toward the infinite, beyond the constraints of linear time. They showed Ahmed the threads of possibility that intertwined with Earth's history—futures where humanity had transcended its limitations, and others where it self-destructed, blinded by the illusion of separateness. For the first time, Ahmed perceived his place within this grand schema: a bridge, a witness, a keeper of awakening. Yet, in that moment, the boundary of his understanding shattered, revealing a universe alive and fluid—a vast ocean of potential currents, flowing and converging in a dance of cosmic probability.

And then, as suddenly as it had begun, the vision receded. Ahmed opened his eyes to find the ruins of the cottage—silent, insistent, waiting. But something had changed within him. Beneath debris and dust, he uncovered a small, crystalline artifact pulsating with an internal luminescence—an unassuming object with a purpose he could barely comprehend. The sun had begun to rise, casting a pale, diffused glow over the landscape, and with it, a profound realization settled deep in his bones: his journey was no longer rooted solely in scholarship or history, but in a sacred responsibility—to recognize the signs, to ignite awareness, and to serve as a guardian of the cosmic keys laid bare within this moment. The landscape itself seemed to echo in silent affirmation—an open door waiting patiently for those daring enough to step through into the infinite.

***

Fourteen

Lawrence's Legacy

Beyond the Myth, Into the Infinite

Darkness stretched its heavy fingers across Bovington Heath, shadows rolling over the rough terrain where the land seemed to breathe in muted anticipation. Ahmed sat atop his battered vehicle, its engine dead in the dusk, yet his mind pulsed with a force that made the landscape appear suddenly alive—as if whispering secrets long buried beneath centuries of gravel and moss. The air was thick with a peculiar stillness, broken only by the distant hoot of an owl and the faint creak of the trees whispering beneath a chilly wind. In that silence, the boundary between understanding and doubt blurred, as though the very land was challenging him to decipher its silent language.

He had come seeking Lawrence's myth, a shadow cast over the desert sands and the corridors of history. Instead, what awaited him was a landscape laced with veils thicker than he had anticipated—mysteries that did not lend themselves to rational discourse or scholarly skepticism. The broken-down vehicle, the worn shoes of his research, suddenly felt like relics of an earlier naivety. Somewhere beyond the horizon, the dim glow of solar lights flickered—an unspoken invitation that seemed to pulse with a life of its own, beckoning him to unravel a truth far beyond academic footnotes. His pulse quickened as a strange premonition stirred; he suddenly sensed layers of time folding over themselves, wrapping around him like a shroud woven from the silent fabric of eternity.

As he watched, a faint shimmer appeared beneath the horizon—a kind of ripple in the air, almost imperceptible yet undeniably present. It was a distortion, like a mirage whispering of hidden dimensions. The landscape around him seemed to shift momentarily, a subtle dance of shadows and light hinting at a realm where linear progression no longer held sway. The air thickened, charged with a momentous presence that pulsated through his bones, stirring memories of the lectures on metaphysical physics he rarely dared to invoke in the sterile halls of academia. Every sense heightened, Ahmed felt himself teetering on the brink of revelation, the boundary between the known and the unknowable dissolving with every breath.

The faint glow blossomed into a radiant hue as suddenly—so swiftly that his eyes almost refused to register it—a craft appeared, hovering silently above the ancient hill that locals only whispered about. It shimmered with a liquid-like iridescence, shifting through states of matter—part polished metal, part translucent liquid, and part something altogether unfamiliar, as if the universe itself had folded into a form of living light. Its contours shimmered under the moon's pale gaze, pulsating in rhythm with the deep currents of unseen energies. In that moment, Ahmed's rational mind struggled to grasp its existence; yet, an intuitive part of him understood that his world was now deeply entwined with something far greater, a confluence of cosmic forces and human curiosity beyond comprehension.

From its shimmering surface, tall beings emerged—formless yet luminous, their figures suggesting evolution perfected beyond the confines of biology. They carried themselves with a serene authority, their presence both calming and overwhelming. Their eyes seemed to pierce through time itself, conveying messages not through words but through a symphony of consciousness transmitting directly into Ahmed's mind. The language was fluid—Arabic, English, even ancient dialects—interwoven seamlessly as if thoughts were threads woven from the fabric of existence. These custodians of the unseen extended a profound invitation: to recognize that the universe's tapestry was woven with consciousness, and that humanity's fragmentary awareness was merely a thin veil over a vast ocean of potential futures. In that instant, Ahmed grasped that Lawrence's secret pursuits had transcended mere military tactics and political ambitions; they had been attempts to interface with the foundational currents of reality itself.

Their presence heralded a state of being that defied physical description—a perpetual becoming, a consciousness unbound by space, color, or form. Across the silent void, they showed him Earth's myriad probability streams, futures seeded with divine promise or catastrophic ruin, depending on human choices. Some timelines saw humanity awakening to its cosmic nature, spreading across galaxies with a collective consciousness that shimmered in unison; others spiraled into chaos, blind to the seas of possibility flowing beneath their feet. The beings explained that Lawrence, with his deep connections to the desert's relentless silence, had indeed ventured into these currents, seeking the knowledge that could unlock mankind's return to the infinite. These currents, they revealed, are not fixed points but fluid pathways—channels through which consciousness could ascend, transforming human perception from linear fallacies into shimmering waves of eternal awareness.

Time lost its hold, dissolving into a liquid realm that ebbed and flowed with infinite possibilities. The beings, luminous and silent, became guides—ancient yet timeless—showing Ahmed that Earth's geomagnetic nodes and hidden ley lines are the anchors of these currents. Lawrence's work, long dismissed as mere adventure, was a map to these intersections—sites where the fabric of time itself thinned like translucent silk awaiting the touch of those willing to cross. Their message was one of responsibility: not to exploit these gateways but to safeguard them, recognizing that each act of awareness influences the very course of human evolution. As awareness rippled through his mind, Ahmed saw that the legacy of Lawrence was far more profound than political stratagems or military exploits; it was the silent calling to shield the thresholds where consciousness could leap across dimensions—an eternal dance with the infinite.

The cosmic custodians showed him visions of civilizations beyond the stars, their minds extending in unison through the grand ocean of time, their existence a testament to evolution's ceaseless hunger for transcendence. They explained that Lawrence's pursuit was not about conquest but communion—a quest to understand the malleability of time and the unity of universal consciousness. They described Earth as a nexus point, a crossroads standing at the verge of a collective spiritual uprising or collapse, depending on whether its inhabitants could recognize the truths lurking beneath the surface of their accepted reality. Ahmed, overwhelmed and humbled, felt his own boundaries dissolve as he entered a space where thought governed matter, and intent shaped future pathways. The revelation was searing—his minds ablaze with the understanding that every moment was a portal, every act a potential gateway to the unfathomable depths of existence.

When awakening gently drew him back to the reality of the ruined cottage, the dawn was breaking—its light cast long, golden shadows across the battered landscape. Yet, within him, a profound shift had occurred. Hidden beneath layers of dust and decay, he discovered artifacts that held the echoes of truth: Lawrence's personal correspondence, sketches of craft undreamt of by any engineer, maps that marked not just geography but the unseen currents threading through the earth. A typewritten page, still faintly warm, revealed Lawrence's final message—more than words, a command to find the Sahra Al-Zaman, the Desert of Time, a shimmering state of consciousness awaiting those brave enough to traverse its currents. In a dusty wardrobe, he uncovered Lawrence's belongings—an odd fusion of military relic and Bedouin robes, a symbol of the crossing between worlds. Their presence suggested Lawrence had been more than an author of rebellion; he had been a guardian, a sentinel who navigated the thresholds, seeking the ultimate understanding of the universe's shimmering fabric.

Most unsettling was a small crystalline device left behind—designed not for practical use but as a key to unlock awareness that surpasses the physical. As Ahmed gazed into its facets, he recognized its purpose: a beacon, a bridge between human consciousness and the eternal currents Lawrence had glimpsed. The final, haunting detail was Edith's journal, where she chronicled his arrival in her archives—decades into the future—her words revealing that the true mission had always been to carry the torch of this esoteric knowledge forward. The image crystallized: Ahmed was now entwined in a mission far beyond scholarly pursuits—he had become a guardian of the thresholds, a vessel through which the silent, luminous beings' ancient work could continue.

As the first light of morning spilled over the landscape, Ahmed felt an inexplicable urgency—an internal compulsion to act, to prepare for the crucial moment when humanity might stand at the edge of its own awakening. The landscape, once merely a place of memory, had become a living symbol of transition; the ruins echoed with the resonance of unseen forces guiding him toward a destiny intertwined with the eternal dance of consciousness. Lawrence's true legacy, now laid bare, was no longer a myth but a living pathway—an invitation to see beyond the surface, to navigate the currents of the desert of time, and to serve as a bridge between the finite and the infinite. With this realization settling deep within, Ahmed stepped forward into the unfolding mystery, knowing that the final act was yet to come—and his role, though shrouded in silence, was pivotal in the grand unfolding of humanity's awakening into the boundless ocean of eternity.

***

In the quiet aftermath of his arrival at the rambling bungalow pressed among the twisted limbs of silver birch and swollen rhododendrons, Dr. Ahmed Ridha felt a strange pulse in the air—an undercurrent that disturbed the normal rhythms of reality itself. The late afternoon sunlight, once mellow and predictable, seemed to ripple, casting elongated shadows that shimmered with a subtle, impossible motion. The house, modest in appearance yet oddly charged with an unspoken presence, beckoned him inward as if waiting for its next visitor—one capable of bridging worlds. Every step he took across the creaking floorboards echoed with the weight of unseen truths, whispering of a realm where linear time unraveled like a frayed cloth, revealing layers of existence hidden beneath the illusion of chronology.

Inside, the air was thick with the aroma of aged paper, exotic spices, and something more elusive—an intangible chemistry that thrummed beneath the surface of the room, resonating with memories long buried in the subconscious of the earth itself. Shelves bowed under the weight of first editions, dust motes dancing like tiny oracles whispering forgotten wisdom, while Persian miniatures and silver trinkets shimmered under the flickering light. Lady Edith Carrington, poised and regal, moved like a woman who had witnessed centuries of history trail through her veins, her eyes holding a universe of stories that seemed to flicker with an otherworldly light. Her presence blurred the line between the past and the present, her voice flowing with quiet authority as she conjured images of Lawrence reciting Quranic verses in perfect Arabic, pacing with an intensity that made the walls seem to vibrate with unspoken power. Her words invited Ahmed into a realm where time was not a continuous march but a mosaic of infinite moments intertwined in ways he had never dared to imagine.

As Lady Edith unfolded tales of clandestine gatherings—men and women whose names echoed through history yet whose actions hovered just beyond the grasp of ordinary perception—the boundaries of rationality gently dissolved. She described Lawrence not merely as a military strategist but as a seeker, a man who wandered through the corridors of history seeking something beyond the visible—an elusive key to understanding the very fabric of existence. These stories, woven with intimacy and punctuated by the gentle clang of her antique tea set, revealed Lawrence's retreat into his private sanctuary, Clouds Hill, as more than an escape from the battlefield. Edith claimed that beneath the guise of solitude, Laurence had been delving into temporal anomalies—phenomena that defied the laws of physics; ripples in the space-time continuum that he studied like a scholar hunting for cosmic secrets buried in the sands of the desert. Her words, slow and deliberate, hinted at a truth far more profound than mere legend—that these anomalies were gateways, gateways to dimensions where past, present, and future converged in an eternal now.

In that moment, her presentation of Lawrence's journals, long thought lost, challenged every certainty Ahmed had before. The leather-bound volumes, now displayed with reverence, betrayed no signs of forgery; their pages brimmed with precise, scientific notation—experimental logs, sketches of peculiar craft, and baffling annotations describing "chronological displacement events." Lawrence's handwriting, flowing yet firm, detailed experiments in perception and consciousness, suggesting that the man who had once strolled across the desert with a rifle in hand was also a clandestine pioneer of what could only be called dimensional navigation. These writings did not resemble military intelligence but rather a clandestine quest into realms that exist beyond ordinary comprehension, where time itself becomes an elastic tapestry, rippling at the touch of a consciousness attuned to higher frequencies.

Edith's revelation about the true meaning behind Lawrence's dedication "To S.A."—which had long been dismissed as an inside joke or affectionate nod—pierced the veneer of scholarly misinterpretation. Her voice lowered, barely above a whisper, as she explained that "S.A." was an abbreviation of "Sahra Al-Zaman"—the "Desert of Time," an abstract construct rooted not in geography but in an esoteric understanding that Lawrence had developed through his immersions in the ancient sands and the mystical currents coursing beneath them. To Lawrence, this was no mere metaphor; it was a concrete reality, a space where Earth's fundamental temporal fabric was malleable—a place where the boundaries of past and future dissolved, revealing a continuum of consciousness accessible only through specific states of awareness. His legendary journeys into the desert's empty vastness, Edith claimed, were explorations of this metaphysical realm—test runs for the ultimate voyage into the consciousness ocean that underpins all existence.

As the shadows lengthened and the dusk deepened into night, Edith's stories transformed from historical anecdotes into visions of something profoundly other. She spoke of her own role as a guardian—a sentinel charged with observing and maintaining the delicate gateways that thread through the terrain of time, watching as beings from beyond the linear dimension drifted in and out of human awareness.

"They are watchers," she murmured softly, "custodians of the currents that flow beneath the surface of our perceived reality. Lawrence was their pupil, and perhaps now, so are you."

Her words sent a shiver through Ahmed, whose skeptical mind struggled to grasp the fullness of what was unfolding. Every logical fiber in him rebelled against the idea that historical figures like Lawrence had pursued truths that transcended history itself, yet the evidence before him—the journals, the artifacts, Edith's calm certainty—held him captive to a different understanding.

Then, at precisely 3:17 AM, Edith's voice shifted, dropping into a tone filled with reverence and anticipation. "This is Lawrence's hour," she said quietly, gesturing toward the open window as if the night itself was listening. A harmonic resonance, soft yet insistent, began to build—a subtle vibration in the air, felt rather than heard. Outside, the sky above Clouds Hill seemed to fracture, revealing flashes of impossible light, like fractured parchment imbued with celestial energy. The fabric of space itself stretched and shimmered, revealing a craft of shimmering liquid-metal that floated just above the ground, its surface oscillating through colors and textures beyond human comprehension. The craft seemed to breathe, its shape folding and unfolding as if alive, projecting an aura of infinite possibility that invited Ahmed to step beyond the limits of sight and sound into a realm where consciousness was the only currency.

Dark forms emerged from the craft—tall, luminous beings radiating a gentle yet commanding presence, appearing to evolve beyond the limitations of skin and bone. They communicated through a direct sharing of thoughts, a fluid language of images and sensations, bypassing words altogether. Duty and curiosity, fear and longing flooded Ahmed's mind as these entities outlined their purpose: to serve as custodians of the conscious evolution of Earth's inhabitants. They explained that the planet was approaching a point of critical transformation—an intersection where awareness and existence would either ascend to new levels or fracture into chaos, depending on whether humankind recognized its own potential. In that instant, Ahmed sensed that the boundaries separating him from these beings, these higher forms of existence, were dissolving, their consciousness merging seamlessly with his own. Time lost meaning in that moment—what remained was a vast ocean of stillness, punctuated by the gentle ripple of higher knowledge flowing directly into his mind.

He perceived Earth's multiple probability streams—possible futures stretching in all directions like shimmering ribbons—some leading to cosmic awakening, others spiraling into destruction born from ignorance and fear. The beings unveiled Earth's fragile position—a nexus point within the infinite fabric of space-time—where conscious choice would determine the fate of humanity's evolution. Their presence, their message, was both an invitation and a warning: to cross the threshold of this cosmic river, humans must embrace a deeper understanding of consciousness, relinquish their attachment to linearity, and awaken to the profound truth that time is an ocean, not a river. As Ahmed's perception expanded, he understood that Lawrence's quest had always been intertwined with this revelation—that the desert was not just a place of physical hardship but a sanctuary of potential, a key to unlocking the hidden depths of the mind. The walls of the bungalow, the artifacts, and Edith's calm voice all echoed the same truth: the journey was ongoing, and the next step belonged to those willing to see beyond what their senses constrained them to accept. When he finally opened his eyes, the night had dissolved into dawn, yet the truths glimpsed stayed vivid—a mirror reflecting the infinite possibilities awaiting the consciousness of humankind.

***

Ahmed's engine coughed a final insubordinate gasp before succumbing to the cold Dorset dusk. The car's sudden stall seemed more than mere mechanical failure—it felt as if the landscape itself had reached out, pulling him into an unforeseen silence. Shadows stretched long across the heath, rippling with an almost perceptible tremor that suggested more than just the settling of twilight. As he sat still, heart pounding and palms clammy, the distant hum of the universe seemed to pause, waiting for something unseen to unfold. The whispering wind carried a faint echo of voices, of tales too ancient or too profound for ordinary ears—memories woven into the fabric of this place, beckoning the awakened child within him to listen beyond noise and rational doubt.

From his vantage point beside the wrecked vehicle, Ahmed's gaze drifted toward the obscured horizon where a rolling field of gorse and silver birch converged in a phantasm of shadows. His thoughts churned—of Lawrence, of Edith, of the whispers that had begun to invade his rational mind. Was this merely the somber allure of a fading day, or something more—the unfolding of a truth that lay beneath the veneer of history and scientific certainty? The air grew heavier, charged with a tension that resonated not with fear but with insistent curiosity. It was as if an unanticipated threshold had emerged, shimmering faintly just outside perception, pulling him forward into uncharted territory that challenged all academic boundaries he had once adhered to. This wasn't just an accident of machinery; it felt like an orchestrated call across dimensions.

In that moment, a peculiar stillness enveloped him. Then, faintly at first, he glimpsed a flicker—like the shimmer of a mirage—a fleeting distortion in the air itself. His senses sharpened; he felt a wave of perceptual dissonance, as if a bridge between realities was momentarily exposed. The landscape shimmered with an internal vibration, and suddenly, the night seemed to pulse with a rhythm that was not his own. Somewhere distantly, the spirit of Lawrence's quest manifested—an echo of ancient pursuits nestled within the Dorset soil, yet reaching far beyond, into realms where the linear unravelled into the infinite. The idea that the landscape held secrets—alive with unseen currents—drew him with an almost magnetic pull. His skepticism faltered as he recognized the fingerprints of forces long buried in myth and silence, now awakening to claim their heir.

As he stood uncertain, a gentle glow emerged from the direction of the old cottage. Light spilled from its windows in delicate pools, casting elongated shadows that danced with urgency—a sign of presence, perhaps, or a beckoning into the heart of that silent sanctuary Edith had described. A figure approached, refined and composed—the elderly woman whose bearing betrayed aristocratic origins in her measured steps and regal poise. Her eyes, bright yet unfathomable, met his with a calm that bore centuries of knowledge. Without a word, she extended a hand, and in that gesture lay the unspoken truth of her role: a guardian of moments slipping through the cracks of linear time, a sentinel of the threshold. Though perplexed, Ahmed felt a dormant part of himself stir—an awakening to the possibility that history's surface merely concealed a vast net of truths, waiting patiently for those capable of crossing into the deeper currents.

Inside, the atmosphere defied the modest exterior, where shelves groaned under the weight of first editions and rare artifacts, whispering of mysteries that defied conventional understanding. Walls adorned with Persian miniatures and artifacts from distant deserts served as silent witnesses to stories that challenged the very notion of linear history. As Edith poured the rare pu-erh, its fragrant steam swirling in the quiet room, she began to speak as if from a realm beyond speech—her words weaving a web of stories layered with subtle symbolism and hidden meanings. She recounted gatherings where Lawrence himself paced before a flickering fireplace, reciting passages from sacred texts in Arabic, while Sassoon, with his sharp analytical eye, scribbled notes and Augustus John sketched restless figures soaked in the glow of moonlit debates. Her voice dropped to a whisper, hinting that Lawrence's retreat to Clouds Hill was more than a simple sanctuary—it was a nexus point in the unknown, a site where the fabric of time itself flickered and warped, twisted by forces beyond ordinary comprehension.

Then Edith revealed the journals—those elusive volumes said to have perished amid chaos or conspiracy. The pages, she insisted, were authentic, each ink stroke brimming with clandestine science and mystical insight. Lawrence's writings portrayed a world where the boundaries of consciousness dissolved, where specific locations became portals—doorways through which the mind could transcend linearity. He had, Edith claimed, documented encounters with phenomena that defied explanation: vessels of light, incomprehensible crafts, and anomalies that teased the edges of space and time. The sketches, too—strange craft with intricate geometries—hinted at a technology that was neither understood nor acknowledged by modern science. For Ahmed, the walls of reason cracked open, revealing glimpses of a universe far richer and stranger than he had ever imagined—a cosmos unbound by the illusion of perpetual progression but woven with the threads of eternity itself.

The core revelation lay in the meaning behind Lawrence's cryptic dedication "To S.A."—not a personal homage, as scholarship long suggested, but an encrypted tribute to Sahra Al-Zaman, the Desert of Time. Edith's voice trembled with reverence as she explained this semi-mystical concept—an axis of the Earth where the currents of time intersected, a place where moments could fold, unfurl, and intertwine. Lawrence, she claimed, had discovered that some locations on the planet served as confluences of these energetic streams, unlocking visions and truths hidden from linear consciousness. The desert, vast and silent, had revealed its secret to him: that time itself was malleable, a thing to be navigated, manipulated by those who dared to understand its language. The landscape's emptiness concealed a profound power—that of awareness piercing through veils of illusion, revealing the fluid, interconnected nature of reality.

As night deepened, Edith's stories took on a luminous quality, transforming the ordinary into the occult. She spoke of her own role as keeper of one such nexus—an eternal guardian overseeing the passage of consciousness through the shifting corridors of time. She described Lawrence's investigations as a quest that extended far beyond military strategy, into the realms of the unseen—a search for the ultimate truth embedded in Earth's very bones. Her tales hinted that Lawrence's retreat was not retreat at all but a voyage into the heart of temporal mystery, with his soul tethered to forces that stretched beyond the confines of space and history. Ahmed's skepticism was dissolving, replaced by an undeniable sense of participating in a grand, multidimensional mosaic—one woven with the threads of consciousness itself. When she spoke of beings from beyond linearity—luminous entities that flickered on the edge of perception—he felt their presence echoing in the quiet corners of his mind, whispering promises of truths yet beyond human grasp.

It was precisely at Lawrence's hour—a heavily charged moment at 3:17 AM—that the air around him thickened, and the fabric of what he knew as reality began to warp. The sky above Clouds Hill fractured into a mosaic of shifting light—like ancient parchment torn and recomposed in impossible geometries. An iridescent craft appeared, shimmering between states of matter; it glowed with a liquid luminosity, blurring distinctions between solid and wave, presence and absence. Tall beings, luminous and ageless, materialized from the shimmering hallways of the cosmos—forms of pure awareness, emerging from the beyond. Their voices—more thought than sound—flooded into Ahmed's mind, speaking fluent Arabic, English, and languages with no origin but which echoed the collective memory of eternity. They declared themselves custodians of consciousness—keepers of the evolution that stretched past human perception—demonstrating that Earth's current crisis was but a crossing point, a moment when humanity teetered on the brink of its greatest leap, or its darkest descent.

What followed transcended words. Ahmed felt himself slipping into a liquid dimension of thought and being, where he was both observer and participant in an ongoing creation—a collective fabric woven from the dreams, fears, and hopes of all conscious life. The entities unveiled Earth's myriad potential futures: alternate streams of existence, some destined for transcendence, others for chaos—timelines where humanity awakens, and others where it sleeps forever in illusions of linearity. They explained that the universe's most profound secret was that consciousness, itself, was the prime creative force—an endless wellspring from which reality flowed and folded back into itself. Time was a vast, flowing ocean, not a river wound tight between banks, and only those trained in the language of awareness could navigate its currents freely. This revelation was both a gift and a burden—Ahmed understood that with this knowledge came responsibility, a duty to aid the collective consciousness in reaching that precipice where evolution becomes inevitable.

When consciousness receded, he awoke alone among the ruins of the cottage, shadowed by the dawn's first light, yet carrying a shard of understanding that could not be unseen. Beneath the debris and dust, remnants of Edith's archives beckoned—letters, maps, journals, and Lawrence's own typewritten notes, each bearing witness to encounters that defied time. He discovered a single sheet of paper in Lawrence's familiar hand, inscribed with ink so fresh it still glistened: "Find Sahra Al-Zaman." The message, in its silence, carried the weight of eternity. In the corner of the room, untouched by grime or decay, lay Lawrence's old motorcycle—pristine, as if awaiting a rider who understood the true nature of journeys. The form of the machine reflected the subtle truth that beneath every surface, beneath every story, lay a portal—an invitation to cross the boundaries of space and mind, into the infinite realm Lawrence had glimpsed and wished others to see. As the early sun cast a pale glow over the landscape, Ahmed realized that the long journey—and his own next step—had only just begun. The secret lay not only in the past but in an unfolding future where consciousness itself would chart a new course—guided by the legacy of Lawrence, now revealed as a guardian of the thresholds, a silent custodian of the beyond, waiting for those willing to step through.

***

Fifteen

Epilogue

The Dawn of the Cosmic Threshold

The first faint blush of dawn seeped through the fractured remains of what once was a cottage, its rays casting fractured shadows across the uneven floorboards. Ahmed stood at the threshold, breath catching in his chest as a sudden ripple of inexplicable stillness surged through the air. His heart pounded not from fatigue but from an awakening that stirred beneath his skin, as if a deep well of consciousness had been tapped and was now spilling into his senses. Every nerve felt attuned to a subtle hum—the echo of a presence beyond the tangible—an intricate symphony that beckoned him forward into a space where past, present, and future coalesced seamlessly.

He stepped cautiously into the interior, the wooden floor cold beneath his feet as fragments of ancient correspondence, weathered yet somehow palpable, cluttered the cluttered space. Among faded photographs and yellowed maps, a worn typewriter—Lawrence's own Underwood—rested like a silent sentinel. His fingers trembled as he brushed over its surface, sensing the weight of unseen histories pressing against him. It was in that moment that the room seemed to exhale, releasing whispers of memories not contained in mere ink, but echoed in the silent language of consciousness itself. Every object, every word, held a fragment of a deeper truth waiting to be unlocked.

It was Edith Carrington's words that later echoed through his mind, guiding him through the fading light and into the depths of a revelation that dissolved conventional boundaries. With deliberate care, she had unfolded the story behind Lawrence's mysterious dedication: "To S.A."—not a simple initials, but a coded homage to "Sahra Al-Zaman"—the Desert of Time. To Ahmed, it was as if the very air vibrated with the significance of the phrase, hinting that time was not a relentless current but an expansive, malleable domain. Edith's stories painted Lawrence as a figure who had glimpsed this realm, a visionary who had pierced the veil of linear history to discover the fleeting edges of a cosmic fabric that stretched beyond comprehension.

Night thickened, cloaking the landscape in a shroud that shimmered with unspoken secrets. Outside, the air now pulsed with an almost imperceptible resonance, signaling the threshold at which science, myth, and consciousness blurred into chaos and clarity. Ahmed felt it—a rising tide of energy that drew him inexorably toward the veranda, where the air shimmered with a silvery brilliance, as if the very fabric of space narrowed or expanded depending on unseen currents. The world seemed to hold its breath, the boundary between known physics and something far more profound dissolving just beyond reach.

Then, suddenly, at precisely 3:17 AM, the silence broke with a harmony that defied auditory explanation, yet resonated viscerally through every cell. The sky above—no longer a mere canopy of stars but a fractured card of luminous shards—appeared to ripple. An entity of impossible luminosity descended from this fractured realm, a figure whose form seemed to flicker between dimensions—tall, shimmering, and fluid. Their presence was both a living memory and an evolving consciousness, a culmination of countless millennia of cosmic evolution. Their gaze reached into Ahmed's mind, bypassing language, resonating directly in the core of his being. The sense was not of foreign intrusion but of awakening—a calling to a higher understanding the mind could scarcely comprehend in its waking state.

These beings, vast yet boundless, spoke without words—a transmission of thought so pure that it felt as if his very soul was being refined and expanded simultaneously. They revealed that Earth itself was a nexus—an intersection point where currents of time, consciousness, and energy intersected with extraordinary precision. It was no accident that Lawrence's retreat had served as more than a refuge; it was a beacon at the edge of a multidimensional crossroads. The guardians explained that humanity was on the cusp of a transition—a crossing into a state of awareness that would unlock the dormant forces annihilating linear time and revealing a universe of endless potential.

Ahmed's perception shifted as he realized that this encounter was not an isolated event, but part of an ongoing cosmic symphony. The beings' collective consciousness described a civilization existing beyond the possessions of matter—an evolving, refining collective that had long ago transmuted into light and thought. They showed him visions of Earth's many possible futures—futures where consciousness had advanced enough to grasp the true nature of existence, and others where darkness descended through ignorance and fear. The weight of responsibility pressed upon him: to remember, to awaken others, and to bridge the gap between linear history and the infinite possibilities that lurked beneath it.

As the dawn threatened to break the horizon, the luminous entities dissolved into waves of shimmering light, leaving behind a lingering resonance that hummed in the depths of Ahmed's mind. He felt an unprecedented clarity, an understanding that the entire universe was a liquid sea of potential—its currents manipulated by awareness, intention, and a consciousness willing to perceive beyond the illusion of separation. His body, once bound by rationalist constraints, now thrummed with the pulse of something eternal—a calling to serve as a guide for others who would dare to cross into this expansive, uncharted territory. The landscape around him, the relics he'd uncovered, even the shadowed ruins, echoed with an urgent message: everything was interconnected, fluid, and alive with meaning.

Still trembling, Ahmed turned from the ruins, clutching a small crystalline fragment—the gift of the guardians—and walking back toward the battered remnants of the cottage. In that moment, a sudden gust of wind swept through the heathland, sweeping away the last vestiges of night, revealing a sky painted with colors that defied description. His mind, flooded with images and sounds from dimensions beyond, felt both shattered and whole—an awakening that could never be undone. The past, the present, and the infinite layers of potential all intertwined within his consciousness now, forever altered. The realization settled: what Lawrence had glimpsed, what Edith had described, was not a myth but a doorway—an invitation to transcend limits and walk into the vast unknown awaiting on the other side of the cosmic threshold.

***

The landscape of human understanding, long governed by patterns of certainty and the illusion of linear progress, begins to tremble as inexplicable disturbances ripple across the fabric of time itself. These anomalies, subtle yet relentless, manifest first as fleeting impressions—an ancient song heard faintly in a distant alley, a familiar scent misplaced in a modern city street—signs that beneath the veneer of normality, unseen currents are stirring. The collective consciousness of nations, often oblivious to the silent upheaval, reveals signs that the threshold separating dimensions is approaching, and history's smooth continuity is flickering like a candle about to be snuffed out. As the world's clocks tick on, synchronized in a rhythm that now seems out of sync, scientists and mystics alike sense that the temporal patterns are shifting in ways that defy rational explanation, unsettling the very notion of cause and effect. The universe whispers through cracks in the known, hinting that the boundaries of time are dissolving, revealing a chaos that holds the promise—or the threat—of rebirth or ruin.

In secluded research institutes and discreet government laboratories, engineers observe fluctuations in electromagnetic readings, anomalies that strain the limits of contemporary technology. Data streams flicker and twist, as if the currents of history itself are distorting, twisting the fabric of the past, present, and future into a tangled skein of possibilities. Some respond with skepticism, dismissing the events as glitches, mere aberrations in the complex choreography of modern science. Yet others recognize patterns emerging—patterns that seem to ripple outward from certain key locations on the globe, like unseen nodes in a vast network.

Among these, specific sites in the Middle East, remote deserts, and ancient temple ruins register inexplicable deviations, their coordinates aligning into a constellation of temporal hotspots. These spots act as gravitational centers for the anomalies, pulling the threads of probability into loops and overlaps. Humanity's collective sense of stability frays, and a quiet, persistent question looms: Are these anomalies mere fluctuations or signs of a cosmic shift—a reordering of the very flow of existence?

At the heart of this unfolding enigma, scholars and mystics find themselves drawn into a shared orbit—each seeking answers in different languages, spiritual beliefs, and empirical methods. Dr. Ahmed Ridha, his mind still reeling from the contentious debate at the Oxford conference, feels an uncanny resonance in these strange occurrences. His background in Middle Eastern history has long been intertwined with memories of ancient myths and oral traditions hinting at gateways between worlds. As evening falls, he notices how the Dorset sky mirrors the turbulence in global consciousness—clouds swirling unpredictably, shadows elongating across the landscape, and the distant crack of thunder echoing the rumbling complexity of the anomalies. Whether rooted in physics or mysticism, there remains a shared intuition that these shifts are nothing short of a fundamental transformation—a passage through the fabric of time that could redefine humanity's understanding of existence itself.

In this restless atmosphere, the line between science and myth blurs further. Whispered reports from across the world speak of devices malfunctioning at critical moments, of people experiencing vivid déjà vu, of unexplained phenomena tearing at the edges of their waking reality. Some recount visions of ancient cities buried beneath layers of time, others claim to have glimpsed landscapes not mapped on any chart—visions that suggest the past and future are converging into a single, less distinguishable entity. Governments issue cautious warnings, and secret factions begin to pool resources, desperate to understand whether these anomalies threaten or herald a new era. As nations grapple with their own fragmentary perceptions, the shadow of a deeper, cosmic pattern deepens—an intricate dance of events hinting at an awakening on a scale that transcends localized disturbance. It becomes evident that the rising elements of this pattern are not isolated sparks but part of an interconnected storm aimed at dissolving the boundaries we rely on to define reality.

Amidst this chaos, individuals attuned to more subtle currents cross paths—seers, scientists, philosophers—each feeling the pulse of something greater stirring beneath the surface. Ahmed, still caught in the aftermath of the Dorset conference, senses that the anomalies pounding at the Earth's temporal layers resonate with an inner truth—a truth not confined to academic theory but alive in the very marrow of the universe. Night deepens as he examines the patterns emerging from his own research, noticing how the data echoes stories from ancient texts, mystical traditions, and lost chronicles. These echoes seem to beckon him to a hidden understanding: that the anomalies are not mere incidents but harbingers of a larger, cosmic event designed to recalibrate human consciousness. The familiar world, with its rigid distinctions, begins to fracture into fragments of possibility, suggesting that within the chaos lies the silent, inevitable approach of a threshold beyond which nothing remains the same. The question persists—are we witnessing the unfolding of a universal secret, or a prelude to chaos from which there is no return?

As the shadows lengthen and the night winds pick up, a series of inexplicable events escalate—the earth trembles subtly, a sudden gust of wind whispers ancient words, and the stars above flicker in unnatural patterns. Somewhere beneath these skies, the threads of time are weaving themselves anew, forming knots that threaten to unravel the fabric of history. The growing pattern of anomalies hints at a deeper design—one that has waited patiently, cloaked in myth and obscured by the veil of linear time. In the distance, a faint, pulsing hum vibrates through the air, audible to only a few tuned into the right frequency. It is as if the universe itself is adjusting its tune, preparing for the moment when the currents will align and the boundaries between worlds will fade. Humanity stands on the precipice, unaware yet complicit in this cosmic dance, as the rising patterns forge a new, unfamiliar horizon—one where the distinctions between past, present, and future dissolve into the silent symphony of the unknown.

***

The first rays of dawn filtered through the fractured remains of the cottage's battered windows, casting a pale, trembling light over the scattered relics of a life intertwined with secrets that defied the rational mind. Ahmed stood motionless amidst the debris, a sudden stillness settling within him as if the very fabric of perception had frayed at the edges, revealing glimpses of something far beyond the world he thought he knew. The air was thick with an unspoken gravity—an awakening suspended in the silence—where the boundary between the known and the unknowable seemed to dissolve into the ether of possibility. His breath caught as the whisper of unseen currents stirred around him, carrying with them echoes of distant worlds, histories fractured and reassembled in the space of a heartbeat.

In that moment, the landscape outside had lost its familiarity; the landscape inside him shifting in tandem. The ruins hummed with a silent energy that seemed to pulse from the very earth beneath his feet, a pulse that beckoned him to listen beyond the surface. Where once he saw only weathered wood and crumbling mortar, now individual grains of sand shimmered with a thousand stories—each grain a fragment of eternity, each shadow a doorway to remembrance. His fingers brushed against a chipped fragment of pottery, but in that touch, memories unfurled like ribbons—visions of Lawrence, Sassoon, and others who had walked these grounds centuries before, their spirits still dancing along the fractured timeline that he was only beginning to comprehend. His senses stretched to encompass what his rational mind was screaming to dismiss, trembling on the edge of revelation.

Suddenly, the air rippled, a subtle yet profound disturbance, and Ahmed felt a rush of consciousness that was not solely his own. It was as if the fabric of time shimmered and buckled, revealing veins of unseen energy threading through the universe—currents of potential that converged at this very point. From the fractured sky above, a luminous presence emerged—an entity shimmering with a light that flickered between solidity and liquidity, fluid as a liquid mirror yet radiant with an internal glow. Its form constantly shifted, revealing glimpses of multiple dimensions simultaneously, a living mosaic of the infinite. As the being's consciousness touched him, images flooded his mind—pathways branching into futures and pasts, all coalescing into a single point of profound clarity: the moment of the cosmic threshold, a gateway where humanity's destiny merged with the vast cosmic flow, awaiting only the conscious choice to step through."

4 July 2025

***